hush little baby

JENNIFER REBECCA

HUSH LITTLE BABY

Copyright © 2020 Jennifer Rebecca

This book is a work of fiction. Names, characters, places, and incidents are the product of the authors' imaginations and are used fictitiously. Any resemblance of actual events, locales, or persons, living or dead, is coincidental.

All rights reserved. Except as permitted under the U.S. Copyright Act of 1976, no part of this publication may be reproduced, distributed, or transmitted in any form or by any means, including photocopying, recording, or other electronic or mechanical methods, without the prior written permission of the author.

Cover Design by
Uplifting Author Services

Editing by
Kayla Robichaux

For more information about Jennifer Rebecca and her books, visit:
www.jenniferrebeccaauthor.com

hush little baby

Life in George Washington Township and the surrounding areas has once again been shaken to its core. Young, unwed mothers are being found hacked to pieces after crude cesareans, and their babies are nowhere to be found.

While overseeing the investigation, Captain Liam Goodnite receives some surprising news that just might give him the push he needs to make the sexy medical examiner, Emma Parker, his once and for all.

Only Emma isn't one to forgive and forget.

Good thing life has taught Lee some tough lessons, and now he's willing to do whatever it takes.

For Sean, always for Sean. I wouldn't want anyone to
be my baby daddy but you. You take such good care
of us and love us spectacularly. It's a beautiful thing
to witness.

And you're so damn cute when you drop your Rs.
Thanks for being the best guy from New Jersey.

hush little baby

prologue

blood

Blood.

There's so much fucking blood. The stuff is everywhere. Dark-red and sticky, it seeps down like fingers reaching for more. It's like a monster in the night, seeking another victim. I haven't seen this much blood and carnage since the last time I was in the desert.

Hell, even Anna's death wasn't this gruesome.

I rush toward her and drop down to my knees. I need to staunch the flow, but there is so much. I'm not sure where to start or how. I pull my cell phone out of my pants pocket and dial dispatch.

"9-1-1, what is the nature of your emergency?" the dispatcher answers. I don't have time to listen for who it is.

Christ. Jesus Fucking Christ, don't let her be dead.

"This is Captain Goodnite, and I need an ambulance at 1431 Poinsettia Drive," I bark into my phone. "It's an emergency."

She's not dead yet. Her eyes blink open at the sound of my voice and then flit around wildly. There is a shock to this kind of trauma. I have seen men on the battlefield not realize they were mortally wounded or missing limbs. *Please don't let her fucking die.*

"Hang in there," I command her and hope to fuck that for once in her life she listens to me. "It's going to be okay." I just hope I can back up those claims.

Today was supposed to be such a simple day. Lunch with my sister, Claire, so she doesn't drive her husband to homicide, and then a quiet dinner at home with my girl. When Claire's contractions at the restaurant ended in an ambulance ride and emergency surgery, I should have known better.

I spent the afternoon and earlier part of the evening at the hospital. Until I had this weird feeling that something was wrong. It's been a long fucking time since I had a gut check. Those instincts saved me more than a few times on missions. Finally, when I could barely stand it, Wes gave me the all-clear on my sister and her kids, so I rushed home.

What I found there will haunt me for the rest of my days.

Fuck me. There's so much blood. My heart pounds in my chest, and I swallow back against the desert that has invaded my mouth. She's still bleeding. I have to stop the bleeding. I cross my arms over my abs and whip my T-shirt over my head. I press it to the wound that gapes open like a gruesome smile. *They didn't even try to stitch her up.*

Her blood is wicking up through my shirt by the time I see the blue-and-red lights flashing on the wall of my living room. She should have been sitting on the sofa in her sweatpants and watching *The Real House-wives* of Something Stupid. She loves those dumb fucking reality shows almost as much as I love to tease her about them.

There's a knock at the door. Thank God.

"We're in here," I call out.

"What do we have?" one of the paramedics asks me as they roll in a gurney.

"Another baby-snatcher victim," I answer.

"Then you need the ME, not us," his partner says.

"This *is* the medical examiner," I inform them. "And she's still alive."

"Fuck," one of them bites out.

"L-Lee," she rasps and licks her dry lips.

"I'm right here, baby," I say as I hold her hand in mine.

"I-i-it was—" she starts before her eyes roll back in her head and her whole body begins to shake.

"She's coding!" one of the paramedics shouts.

"Sir!" the other one barks at me as he tries to push

me away from her body. "Sir, you have to get back."

I scoot back a foot or two so they can work, and I draw my knees up to my chest. I feel a hand on my shoulder and look up into the understanding eyes of Detective Jones. He thinks she's going to die, but I haven't come this far to give up now.

She can't die on me. I just got her back in my life, got to feel the warmth of her skin pressed against mine, the sounds of her laughter, the sight of her in my house, and the dreams of a future. A future that, as I take in the scene around me, is starting to go missing.

My name is Captain Liam Goodnite, and I'm going to get my family back. I'm going to do whatever it takes.

one

Three weeks earlier...

My heart clenches in my chest. And it hurts like fuck.

I would ask how this became my life, but I know. It's my own damn fault, and it's not like me to blame my issues on other people. But that doesn't mean that when I see Emma walk into a restaurant in a cute-as-hell dress that shows off her growing belly, on the arm of someone else, that it doesn't hurt. Because it does.

It should be me whose arm she's on, and it should be my baby that's growing in her belly, not his. That asshole is living the life that should be mine, and it's no one else's fault but mine.

I was too comfortable in my bachelor ways. I focused on my career with the George Washington Township Police Department. My only goal was filling my dad's shoes and making him proud. That and keeping my baby sister from getting killed. She has always had a penchant for finding trouble, and as much as I've discouraged her from a career in law enforcement, she's damn good at it. I'm proud of her. I can also breathe a sigh of relief, because she's on desk duty now that she's the size of a house with her own pregnancy.

Not that I was making him proud when I distracted myself by keeping company with just about every willing female who crossed my path. And then I hooked up with Emma. I never would have done it, but there was something about her shitty attitude and her ridiculous Metallica T-shirts that make my cock hard. It was after our night together turned into another and another that I realized it's her.

She's the one.

She's a brilliant doctor and she knows it. Her confidence is sexy as all get out. And she hates my fucking guts. I shouldn't be surprised about that one either, not with the way things ended between us. Before I ever slept with Emma, I shared a night, just one, with her friend Anna, not knowing my sister's other best friend harbored secret deep feelings for me that I didn't share.

Anna was sweet and charming, but she wasn't the one for me, and no matter how much I tried to tell Emma that, she refused to listen. Her love for her friend was deeper than anything she might feel for me.

And then Anna died.

Not only did she die during an investigation, but

she didn't need to. She was so desperate to have my feelings reciprocated that she took dangerous risks with a serial killer to prove herself, and it cost her her life.

The guilt after something like that is unbearable. For Emma, it was tenfold. She feels like we're responsible for the actions Anna took at the end of her life. And because of that, we don't deserve to be happy—her words, not mine.

"You can't avoid me forever," I whisper softly from just behind her.

"It would be a lot easier if you played along," she snarks. Holy fuck, how her mouth can make me hard. I want Emma to dress me down every day for the rest of my life so that I can fuck her out of her bad mood afterward forever.

"I can't do that, baby," I admit. "I need you too much."

"No."

"And I think you need me too," I tell her. There's no denying it. Emma and I are like gasoline and matches. We can't help but come together, and when we do, it's incendiary. It's only a matter of time before we fall together again, and when we do, I'm done running, and so is she. She just doesn't know it yet.

"No," she whispers.

"And I think you're scared to fall," I say softly as

I put my hands on her shoulders and gently turn her around to face me so she can see the truth in my eyes. "But I'll catch you, I promise."

"What if you don't?" she asks, and I can hear how scared she is in the tone of her voice, and maybe a little drunk too, if I'm being honest.

"You have to trust me," I tell her.

"I can't."

"Just for tonight," I plead, and I think we both know it's a lie. Once I have her again, I won't be able to let her go. "Just trust me for tonight, and we'll go from there."

"Okay," she replies softly.

"Okay?" I ask, hoping I heard her right over the sound of the waves crashing on the shore.

"Okay," she repeats.

I smile. I've been smiling all night. It's my sister's wedding, after all, but now, it's like all the pieces of the puzzle clicked into place. I'm finally getting everything I ever wanted, and I'm so fucking happy.

I don't care if it's the champagne or the moon over the beach; whatever it was that made Emma Parker agree to a night with me, I'll take it, and I'll keep on taking it, because I am so in love with her. I'm going to use every day for the rest of my life to show her just how much.

We belong together.

She looks up at me and realizes we've slowly moved

out of the light shining from the reception and down to just under the pier. It's dark here and a little secluded. The music from the party can be heard just barely. And it's just us out here.

And in that moment, I want Emma like I have never wanted anything in my life.

"Don't look at me like that, Emma," I warn, my voice strained by my need for her, and so is my cock. "You have to decide now because I can't walk away like a gentleman when you look at me like that."

"Like what?" she asks. She's looking at me from underneath her lashes and bites her lip.

"Like you want me. Like you need my cock like you need air to breathe. Like you want me to make that pretty pink pussy of yours come," I tell her.

"Yes," she breathes as I back her up and her shoulders hit one of the wooden posts of the pier. "I want that. All of it."

"Emma," I plead with her. I need her too much, and her name rolls off my lips like a prayer.

"I want that," she says, bolder than she normally is with me in the bedroom. My cocky, headstrong doctor is a little shy with me behind closed doors. Maybe it's the fresh air. "I want your cock, and I want you to make me come. And I want you."

"Fuck," I bite out before crashing my mouth down on hers.

My kiss is fierce and powerful, and I let that fire

build and consume us both. She lets out a whimper, and I take the opportunity to sweep my tongue inside her mouth and taste all her sweetness. She sucks it deep, letting mine brush over hers as I plunge it in and out of her waiting mouth. And it's fucking heaven.

"Lee," she pleads when I rip my mouth away so we can both drag in a ragged breath.

Slowly, so painfully slowly, I slide the skirt of her dress up, bunching it in my hand as I go. When it's up above her hips, exposing her delicate pink panties, I slide the damp material aside and plunge two fingers into her pussy.

"So wet for me," I say softly.

"Yes," she agrees as she leans her weight back on the post, and her knees begin to buckle, making me smile wickedly.

"Are you going to come for me like this, or do you want my cock in that pretty pussy of yours?" I ask. And we both know she'll come on my hand like this if I keep it up.

"I want your cock," she says honestly.

I unbutton the front of my suit slacks. My hard length springs free, and I revel in the hungry way she watches me, the way she openly wants me. I want all of it. All of her, her heart, her body, her fucking soul, because she owns every fucking part of me. And I'm going to give everything I have to her. In this moment, I won't take whatever she's willing to give. I'm going to take it all.

"That's my girl," I growl. "Lift your leg around my hip. That's it."

I pull the at the seam of her panties over her pussy and to the side and slide my cock all the way in. I lift her up, bracing my hands under her ass so I can lift her up higher and then drive her down over and over again.

"Oh, God," she moans as I slide her up so that only the tip is inside her, and then I power her back down again.

"That's it," I praise as she clenches around me.

"I-I'm going to—" She gasps as her orgasm rolls over her like a steamroller. "Lee!

I pin her to the post, giving her most of my weight, and pump once, twice more... before calling out her name into the night as I follow her over the edge. "Emma!"

I hold her in my arms against the wooden post as we both struggle to catch our breath. I lean my forehead against hers and breathe in her air.

"So what are you doing for the rest of tonight?" I ask her, when really I mean, What are you doing for the rest of forever?

"I had grand plans to go bum a smoke from one of the valet guys," she admits, and I smile against her mouth. That's my wild girl, always looking for trouble.

"Well, seeing as they've all gone home for the night, how about you come back to my room with me

instead?"

"I suppose I could do that," she says hesitantly.

"Excellent," I whisper, not wanting to scare her with my enthusiasm for her.

I set her on her feet and wait for Emma to regain her balance, and then I take her hand in mine and we walk down the beach and back up to the resort where I let us into my room, and we spend another night together.

And this time, I have no plans to let her go.

For six weeks after Claire and Wes's wedding, I held the woman of my dreams in my arms. She was in my bed every night, and I thought we were finally headed in the right direction, one of healing and forgiveness and moving on, but I was wrong. I was so fucking wrong. So here I sit in the bar, drinking scotch and eating alone while the woman I love sits at a table across the room, sharing a meal with someone else.

"Here's your dinner," the waitress says as she leans just a little too close to me, her breasts just under my face.

"Thanks," I murmur, looking up to catch Emma's heartbroken face. I have no idea what she has to be heartbroken about; she's the one who left me for this tool. I'm sure he's a perfectly nice guy and all, but he's not me, and she chose him. That cuts deep.

"And uhh…." She nervously bites her lip before

releasing it. "Here's my number. I, uhh… I get off at eleven if you're free."

"Thanks," I tell her.

I should take her up on her offer. Take her back to her place and give her the night in bed she's promising me, but I can't. I can't, because looking into the wounded eyes of the one woman I want more than anything and can't have ruined any chance of a hard-on I might've been able to work up for this girl.

Thankfully, my phone rings, saving me from making another monumentally bad decision.

"I have to get this; it's work," I explain to her as I shift and pull my cell phone out of my pocket.

"Sure," she says, looking a little dejected. "I'll let you get to it."

"Goodnite," I answer.

"Captain Goodnite, this is dispatch. We have a body."

Looks like I'm saved by the homicide.

two

where's the baby

"Captain Goodnite, this is dispatch. We have a body."

"Where's the location?" I ask as I pull out my wallet and leave more than enough money to cover the meal I'm not going to get to eat and probably won't want once I'm done. Or maybe I will, but it'll be long gone by then. The life of a police officer is never dull.

"The apartments at 241 Ashland," the dispatcher informs me.

"I'm on my way."

I drop the stack of bills and the pretty waitress's number on the table and head for the door. I'd like to think I wouldn't call her, that I've learned my lesson where my heart and my dick are concerned—because if I can't have the one woman my heart wants, I shouldn't offer my dick to anyone else. But who knows how weak I'll be after another month of watching her with that pencil-dicked little weasel? It's hard to say how low I'd stoop when my loneliness consumes me late at night.

I grab my leather jacket off the hook on the side of the booth I was sitting in. That's one of the things I love most about this restaurant; it's open late—which is convenient, because I seem to live at the station lately—and it has these quiet booths in the back of the bar where no one bothers you, but you can see all the exits from here.

I slide my arms in, the lining worn soft from years of wear and tear, but it's still my favorite. I can't seem to slide into the suit completely like Wes did. I wore a uniform for as many years as he did in the military, but then when we came back to Jersey, he went off to the FBI in Quantico, and I came here to wear a different uniform with the police department. Now that I'm the captain, a uniform isn't required anymore, and I strangle myself every morning with a shirt and tie, but that's as far as I'll let it go. This jacket was my grandfather's from when he was a crew chief on navy helicopters.

As I make my way through the restaurant toward the exit, taking care to give Emma and her date a wide berth, I see her out the corner of my eye as she reaches into her bag and pulls out her phone. I push out a frustrated sigh. There's a part of me that hates that we work for the same small township, and there's another more twisted part of me that loves it, because even if I can't have her, she still exists in my world. I get to see her and talk to her, and it's not enough, but it's all I'll ever get. And it's more than I fucking deserve, so I take it like the little bitch I am.

I push open the heavy glass door and hear the bells overhead chime as I head out into the night and toward another tragedy. I tug at the knot of my tie to loosen it as I make my way through the parking lot toward my SUV. This life can take a toll on you, more so now that my sister is on desk duty.

I beep the locks on my department-issued SUV and climb in. I key open the lock on the glovebox and pull out my sidearm and badge, setting both on the dash before I fire up my car and head out of the lot and into the night.

I drive through the gates of the apartment complex. Yellow streetlamps light my way as I circle the building and lead me to the pinnacle of where red-and-blue streaks of light flash into the dark night. It's like the northern lights meets the harbinger of doom. I pull in behind them in a long line of black-and-whites and a crime scene van. The medical examiner, or ME, isn't here yet, but I'm sure she will be soon.

I push open my door, and a heavy feeling settles around me like clockwork. Every case like this seems to mark another piece of my soul. I reach for my badge and holster as I step down from the Tahoe and clip both to my belt before making my way up the sidewalk, my long legs eating up each step that stands between me and whatever tragedy I'm about to walk into.

"Hey, Jones," I say, shaking the young detective's

hand. "What do you have for me?"

"Hey, Cap," he greets me. "Victim is the occupant of the apartment. Nineteen-year-old Ashley Horner. Waitress at the Silver Streak Diner, expecting her first child."

As Jones ticks off each item on his list while he describes the victim, my stomach sours and bile rises up in the back of my throat. Unfortunately, I know exactly what's coming and why Jones—my sister's newest partner, one she hasn't managed to maim or send screaming into the night yet—and I were called out here tonight. We had a case just like this two weeks ago. The girl's life story seems to match this evening's victim's. She had no family, no baby daddy in the picture, and a crap job. If this girl is like the first, she had absolutely no one and nothing to see her through life, and now she doesn't even have that.

"Estimated cause of death?" I ask as we climb the last step to the upper-level apartment just before we cross the threshold.

"Exsanguination," Jones says quietly, his words leaving another mar on my soul. "She bled out."

"And where's the baby?" I ask him, even though I already know what he's going to say. I take the plastic booties one of the crime scene guys hands me and slip them over the soles of my boots, and all it takes is one look to know why. The crappy beige carpet of every cheap apartment there ever was is the same flooring of Ashley Horner's humble abode, but this particular batch is absolutely soaked with blood. It's a horror scene it's so gruesome.

"Gone."

"Fuck," I bite out as I rip a pair of latex gloves from my jacket pocket and start tugging them on.

"Yeah," he says, doing the same.

"Do we know who called it in?" I ask, and by the look on his face, I'm glad I didn't have time to eat the dinner I ordered.

"The downstairs neighbors," Jones answers. "It appears they had a ceiling leak for a few days before the super would take a look."

"Sounds like a great guy."

"No joke," he replies.

"And the neighbors?" I ask.

"Moving, but I have their contact info."

Jones and I move quietly throughout the apartment as we catalogue all the different pieces of Ashley Horner's life. A lot of people would believe the life of a detective is fast-paced and full of action, but they would be wrong. Most of the time, it's combing through the minutiae of the lives of people you will never meet, mostly because they're dead.

It's a lot for one person to handle, and more than enough good cops succumb to their demons, whether it be night terrors, the bottle, or even their own bullet. My sister thinks she's the only one with nightmares and for years hid the fact that she was struggling with the demons leftover from her kidnapping. Claire suffered alone for so long, but what my baby sister didn't know—hell, she still doesn't—is that I've been struggling too.

Not every night, but lately, more often than not, the ghosts of the past come calling when I lie down at night. And I can't help but wonder if one day I won't be able to pretend like they don't exist anymore.

"Hey, guys," Emma says from the front of the apartment. "What did I miss?"

She's zipped up coveralls over her clothes. The material hangs loose over her frame except for where it stretches across her swollen belly. Heavy rubber boots are pulled up to her knees, and her dark-blonde hair with its dyed pink ends are wadded up on top of her head in a glorious mess. *She's* a mess, and yet I've never seen anything more beautiful than her in this state in my entire life.

I don't realize I'm staring until Detective Jones elbows me in the ribs. Sometimes when she's in the room, I feel lost, and the only thing to light my way home is her.

"Looks like another baby snatcher," Jones fills in for me.

I clear my throat, but I don't trust the words that will come out of my mouth yet, so I keep my teeth clenched tight and just nod.

Emma steps into the room. Her assistant raises a camera to her face and snaps picture after picture while Emma crouches down to get a good look at the body.

She pulls the victim's clothes away from her body, and I have to look away. The gaping wound across the young woman's abdomen splits wide like a malicious smile. Her eyes are dimmed in death.

"There doesn't seem to be any blunt force trauma, no GSW or otherwise. Best guess until I get her to my lab is another cesarean."

"I was afraid you'd say that," I admit.

She shrugs. "It's the most likely guess."

I push out a frustrated breath and barely keep myself from shoving a hand through my dark hair. It's a rookie move, and the field guys have been waiting for Ole Cap to make one, like running my hands through my hair while I'm wearing contaminated crime scene gloves.

Jones smirks, because he knows it's a gesture I make all the time and it's killing me to hold back now. Emma bites her plump, light-pink lip to keep from laughing, and her assistant looks away.

"Not today, guys," I say, rolling my eyes. "You're not going to get the goods on Ole Cap today."

"Sure thing, Captain," Emma's assistant, Maryann, says.

"So what else do you assholes have for me?" I laugh.

"Time of death was probably forty-eight hours or so ago," Emma answers me. "I'll know more when I get her in the lab and get a body temp, but rigor has come and gone."

"You're the body expert," I say offhandedly.

"Now, I thought that was you." Emma smiles and winks to take the sting out of her words.

"Ready?" Maryann asks.

"Yeah, let's load her up on three," she agrees. "One… two… three." And then they get the body in the bag and on the board for transport.

"Here," I say, stepping in to lift Emma's end of the board. I don't like that she's doing all the heavy lifting. I know she's capable; hell, Emma is one of the toughest women I know, and I find it sexy as hell, but still. If I can lighten her load, whether she's pregnant or not, I will.

"Thanks," she says as she tucks a finger in the edge of her glove and folds it over, sliding her hand out. She loops it through the edge of the second one, balling them both up without ever touching her hands. We all do the best we can, but somehow Emma makes the move look almost delicate.

I look to Maryann, and we lift the board, carrying Ashley Horner between us down the stairs. Emma beeps the locks on the van she uses to move the deceased back to her morgue. It's a large, nondescript panel van, but honestly it wouldn't surprise me if she showed up one day driving an old hippie van with a unicorn painted on the sides.

Maryann and I slide the board onto the gurney waiting inside, and Emma slams the doors shut before turning to face me.

"I… uhh, I'll just meet you back at the lab," Mary-ann says before scurrying away. Her exit is awkward and a little embarrassing for all of us. Rumors about Emma and me had caused more than a few department tongues to wag.

"Thanks for all your help, Lee," Emma says with a soft smile and a gentle hand on my bicep. The muscle flexes involuntarily under her touch, and I can't help but lean toward her.

"It was nothing," I reply, sounding like a chump, when all I want to do is tell her that I would do anything for her, that the loss of her in my bed these last months has been brutal but were still nothing compared to the distance she's kept.

I brush a dark-gold curl back from her face with the calloused tips of my fingers, and she jumps at the contact, almost as if she'd forgotten where she was and who she was with.

"I should go," she says softly, and I catch her by her arm. Not tight, I would never hurt her; I just want her to give me a little more of her time. I want to understand the mixed signals she's sending me.

"What are we doing, Em?"

three

"I-I-I don't know," she says, and I can see her pulse flutter in the side of her slim neck like a butterfly's wings. "Nothing."

"This doesn't feel like nothing, Emma. Don't you feel it too?" I lean in closer to her and watch her eyes dilate. As much as she wants to claim she doesn't feel anything for me, it's a lie.

"It doesn't matter what I feel," she hisses, and I know I've hit a nerve. I can't push her much farther than this tonight, and I won't risk her health or her baby. I'm greedy where she's concerned, but what I feel for her is big enough to put her basic needs before any wants of my own.

Emma and I keep coming back to this moment time and time again. I love her, and she loves me, but it doesn't matter. It never will, because there's a ghost standing between us, and there always will be. Emma is never going to be able to move on from the loss of her friend, Anna. And life has taught me that you have to honor the fallen and then move on. Grieving for eternity over the lost and refusing to live your life is not honoring them in any way. And no matter what I say or do, Emma will never cave on this.

I push out a heavy sigh and run my hand through my hair like I longed to do when I had gloves on. I can't keep doing this, and I can't stay away. I love her, but I always end up hurting her. I don't know what to do.

"Have a good night, Emma," I tell her as I back away. "Drive safe."

I see she wants to say more, but I can't. I need to let her go, but the hope that one day she'll be mine might be all that keeps me going on the darkest of days.

I turn around and walk back to my car without watching her climb into her SUV, never knowing that the saddest look in the world crossed her beautiful face and that, with the back of her hand, she dashed away a tear before climbing in her van and driving back to the morgue. Instead, I beeped the locks on my Tahoe and climbed in.

I drove out of the little apartment complex on Ashland and back across town to where my old house full of history sits at the top of a small hill. I pull into the driveway and turn off the engine before stepping down.

I shut the car door behind me with just a little too much force, a surefire sign that my frustration is at its peak and it's time for me to call it a night before I do something stupid, and at thirty-nine years old, I am too old to do stupid shit anymore.

I walk up the narrow stone walkway to the door on the front of my house that lets into an all-seasons porch. I unlock the door and step inside, locking it behind me before moving on to do the same thing with the front door. You don't help put away some of New Jersey's worst offenders without learning to be careful, but any innocence I had left was lost when I was sixteen and my baby sister was stolen from our yard by a monster. Somehow, she managed to escape, but not without scars on all our souls. Since then, I've learned to be cautious when needed and more overprotective than I should be. But I can't help it. She had wanted to follow Wes and me around, and I didn't want to babysit. If I would've just included her, she wouldn't have been kidnapped. Maybe if I hadn't pushed Emma so hard, Anna wouldn't have doubled down on her efforts to prove herself and gotten killed.

At the end of the day, the facts don't lie. I'm nothing but a curse for the women in my life.

I strip off my leather jacket and hang it on a hook by the front door before making my way up the stairs to my bedroom that overlooks the driveway. There are several bedrooms upstairs, but my need to be alert and ready won out when I was choosing a space of my own. I worked hard on this house, turning a second bedroom next to the master into an en suite bathroom.

I kick off my boots by the door and lock my badge

and sidearm in the safe I keep in my nightstand drawer. I make my way into the bathroom and turn the shower on. I strip off my clothes and drop them in the hamper before stepping under the spray. I could have used a hot shower to loosen my muscles, but my cock thought otherwise. What couldn't even muster so much as a twitch in the direction of the willing waitress now flares to life for a woman I had in my life and in my bed for six beautiful weeks, and then she was just… gone.

I lather soap all over my body and will my erection to go away, but it's no use. Emma is better than any blue pill. All it takes is one look at her or the sound of her husky voice or even the faint strawberry scent of her shampoo, and I'm hard enough to pound nails.

Fuck it. I'm so hard it hurts, and if I don't do something about it, I'll never get to sleep. I brace my left hand on the cool tile of the shower wall and run my other hand down my face. I hate that I need her like this. I hate that she won't give us the chance to move on and make a life together. I hate that I'm so fucking weak where she's concerned.

I let my hand slide down from my face to my neck and feel the muscle and tendon underneath my fingers. Trailing farther over my chest and the flat abs that take more work and determination at almost forty than they did at twenty, my hand moves down even more until I wrap my fist around the base of my cock and squeeze.

The groan that falls from my lips couldn't be stopped if I wanted it to as I stroke myself from root to tip. I close my eyes and let my head tip backward.

I have no strength in me to hold it up anymore as I see her the last time she was in my bed in my mind. The pink tips of her breasts as they bounced when she demanded that I fuck her harder and I did. The rough moans she made when she was about to come, and even the way her deep-blue eyes stared up at me with hunger as her lush pink lips wrapped around my cock and she sucked me off in this very shower. The way she grabbed the back of my thighs and held on when I tried to get her to pull back so I could fuck her like we both wanted. She wouldn't let me. The way she loved bringing me to my knees and the roar that was ripped from my chest as she swallowed every last drop of me, and the sexy smirk on her face after. And the way that smirk slid right off her face when I gently tipped her back right in the middle of the huge walk-in shower while I licked every inch of her sweet pussy.

The taste of her was still on my lips when I climbed over her and slid deep inside. She was hot and tight and everything I ever wanted in the way that she raised her hips to meet mine as I plunged into her over and over. And when she reached that point of no return, she clung to me while she came, and watching her was by far the most erotic experience of my life.

I let the waves of her climax flow over me as I drove deep inside her. The tile floor abrading my knees, but I didn't fucking care, because she was coming again, and it was just as glorious as the last time, yet this time, I let it carry me away.

I groan as hot ropes of my cum hit the shower wall,

reminding me that what I want most I still don't have. The only thing left of my time with Emma are just memories, ghosts that haunt and won't let me go.

I rinse myself and then the shower wall quickly before grabbing a towel from the rack and drying off. The heaviness of the day finally sinks into my bones and leaves me with an exhaustion that only a three-month hibernation will cure. One look at the clock shows me that I'll have to settle for four hours instead, so I make my way to the bed and pull back the covers. I flop down on the mattress and pull the blankets up to cover me.

And then, blessed sleep claims me, but not for long.

Eyes.

The smell of sulfur fills my nostrils, and smoke sears my lungs. The heavy weight of the rifle in my hands is like second nature to me. I could carry it in my sleep. During training, I probably did.

But it's the eyes that chill me to the bone in the middle of this hot desert.

I don't know how the intel had gone so bad. I know it happens, but not like this. One minute, the mission was going to plan, and the next, the world exploded. Spurts of gunfire can be heard all around me, but it's the screams that ring in my ears.

"Fuck, fuck, fuck!" I hear Adams scream through the comms in my ear. "They're dead. They're all dead."

And he's right. They're all dead. Every last one of them. I was helpless to prevent this, but still I feel like I should have. It's as bad as if their blood was directly on my hands.

I make my way through the village we've been watching, my heart in my throat. Buildings, homes, the carts in the market, they're all gone, burned out shells of what they were before. And bodies are crumpled where they fell. Men, women, children—death does not discriminate. Their eyes vacant after life left them.

If eyes are the windows to the soul, then this is a portal to hell as I look at the faces of each person who should not have died. A child we gave a candy bar to yesterday, an old lady who offered coffee in the market, and a beautiful young woman whose belly was swollen with a baby.

Her dark eyes watch me, haunt me, as she sees me but nothing at all. And then they change to the brown of Ashley Horner's, her belly cut open and her child just gone. I was helpless to stop her death too. I didn't know her, and she still died.

The smoke burns my throat as I turn to the left and see Emma's blonde-and-pink hair, her blue eyes open and watching me, her beautiful body mutilated, because I was in her life.

"No!" I shout.

But the eyes of the dead scream that this is all my fault.

four

Air rushes into my lungs as I sit up in bed and hold my head in my hands, my arms braced on my thighs.

I had the dream again. But this time, it's changing, morphing into a nightmare I don't know how to overcome. The irony of the clusterfuck that my life has become is not lost on me. I sent my sister Claire to Dr. Anna Garner, the department shrink, for her psyche evaluation when she put her name in the running to be promoted to detective. I thought Claire would flunk her tests with flying colors, having no idea that my baby sister was a mastermind at hiding her real trauma.

What I hadn't expected was the two to become friends.

One night, when her on again, off again undercover-cop boyfriend had finally left her for good, Anna and I drank too much and then I took her back to her place to fuck like bunnies. Something I regretted immediately, not because Anna wasn't an amazing human being, but because she was hurting, and she deserved better. And also because I had never crossed the line of sleeping with a colleague before. All around, it was a low douchebag moment of mine, and I'm not proud of it.

What I also did not know was that one night would become the catalyst for feelings Anna harbored for me, feelings I did not return. And also feelings no one knew about, because she kept them locked away until after Emma and I had fallen into bed together and didn't want to climb back out.

There was always a spark with Emma that I could never find with anyone else and probably never would. Her mind is fascinating. She's brilliant and funny, and I could talk to her for hours and then just be quiet with her for even longer. Emma is the total package. If I could describe the perfect woman for me, it would be her.

Emma Parker is the one.

But it was a tangled web I had no idea I was weaving. And the house of cards would soon come crashing down.

I had no idea Anna would become frantic to hold my attention and had intentionally inserted herself between Emma and me. It was desperation she felt to belong somewhere to someone. It was that wild need that got her killed.

But I will never forget hearing Anna beg with her

last words that Emma love me like I loved her, and Emma denied it. Since then, our working relationship has been awkward at best.

A quick glance at my phone shows it's about an hour before my alarm should go off, and the way my heart is still racing from my nightmares proves I won't be going back to sleep. So much for four hours.

I kick out of the tangle of sheets and my towel I kept wrapped around me after my shower, having been so tired that I just fell into bed. I prowl to my closet and pull on a pair of workout shorts and slide my feet into socks and running shoes. I grab my phone and my earbuds and head down the stairs to punish my body in my basement gym.

I pop my earbuds in and crank up the music before punching all the buttons on my treadmill. My life feels like everything is an unbearable uphill climb lately, and so can my run.

"Dammit, Goodnite!" I shout from where I'm standing in the small kitchenette in the station. I was pouring myself a cup of the dark tar we call coffee when my very pregnant sister paraded by with a huge smile on her face and a duty belt wrapped precariously around her big belly.

The minute I saw her, I was so distracted by her newest stunt that I poured coffee all over my hand, scalding the skin. I dropped my favorite mug on the floor, shattering it. Although "favorite" is a term I use loosely about coffee mugs, because I seem to break so many of them on the regular.

I grabbed a paper cup from the cabinet and filled it with coffee before stalking back to my office. I couldn't help but notice all the faces that watched me lose my shit over my sister with excited and gleeful looks all over their faces.

"Get back to work!" I shouted as I stomped through my office doorway. I hoped when I got here this morning that I would be able to sneak in, pound another pot of coffee in the hopes of shaking the cobwebs loose, and get to work. Instead, I noticed the mountains of paperwork on my desk. I hate paperwork, and I hadn't had nearly enough sleep to handle all the bureaucratic bullshit that comes with the job, so I slung my leather jacket over the back of my chair and avoided it like the grownup I claimed to be.

I made my way into the small kitchen fully prepared to lick the burned coffee to the bottom of the pot. I was so desperate for caffeine, and luck was on my side; there was a full pot. I was just pouring a cup of fresh coffee, which finding in the station was akin to winning a multi-state lottery, when my sister pranced through with her new "uniform."

While maternity regulations had her discreetly armed while on desk duty, it did not provide for a full duty rig including baton and taser, which is something Claire knows. However, she's fucking bored. Our mean old grandma always said, "Idle hands are the devil's playground, so wash these dishes before you masturbate and blind the baby angels." I'm thinking the same rules apply to Claire on desk duty.

"You wanted to see me, Cap?" she asks sweetly while peeking her head around the mostly closed door to my office. I swear one day I'm going to have a stroke at my desk, and it'll be all her fault.

"Get in my office now."

"You… uhh… need something?" she prompts, and I can see the hamster on the wheel in her head trying to work her way out of this newest stunt.

"What are you wearing?" I ask, my voice calm and even, which throws her. Claire's eyes widen a fraction before she schools her face.

"Hey, man," Wes says as he walks into my office. My FBI agent best friend and new brother-in-law was bound to make an appearance when he got back from D.C. I knew he'd show soon enough, because bad news never waits. "Hey, baby, I didn't expect to see you here so soon. Get called to the carpet early?" He laughs before getting a good look at her.

I just wait for the other shoe to drop. So does Claire, as she bites her lip. Fortunately, we don't have to wait long, and I feel my face split with a maniacal grin as her husband realizes she's been up to no good the whole time he's been gone.

"What the hell are you wearing?"

"A… uhh… desk sergeant rig?" she asks. I hate the way she manages to answer a question with a question when she knows someone won't like the answer she has to give. Marriage had mellowed her—*some*—but there was still a lot of wild and recklessness in my baby sister. Luckily, Wes could handle what she dished out.

"Jesus Christ, Claire," he bites out. "You're pregnant with twins. You're supposed to be on desk duty."

"I am!" She throws her hands up over her head.

"Really?" Wes barks. "Because it looks like you're carrying more equipment than you need to, and you know the doctor said you were two seconds away from bed rest."

Looking considerably chastised, Claire shrinks before us, looking so much like she did as a little girl and not a thirty-year-old woman who I can't help but rush to her defense.

"Now, she wasn't that bad while you were gone," I tell Wes, making Claire's violet eyes, the ones just like mine, narrow on me.

"That's all you've got?" she snaps, showing it was all an act. Claire is a hot mess, but I love her, and for the most part, she really is harmless. "I wasn't 'that bad'? Really, Lee? Some brother you are."

"I'm the brother who loves you and is tired of seeing you in hospital beds," I say gently.

"Oh all right," she says. "I love you too."

"At least she didn't meddle in your love life while I was gone." Wes laughs, but it's cut short when he notices the sheepish grin on his wife's face.

"What did you do?" I ask.

"Nothing really," she hedges.

"Claire," Wes drawls firmly. "What did you do?"

"Well, they're never going to get their shit together."

"That's not for you to decide," he says.

"But they're doing it all wrong."

"You promised," he reminds gently.

"I lied."

"I'm getting that." He stalks toward his wife. "You're just lucky I think it's sexy how bad you lie. And I missed you."

"If you could take your foreplay with my sister out of my office, that would be great," I say, rolling my eyes.

"No can do, brother. I have to brief you on Palmer's death."

I sigh and push a giant stack of paperwork that needs to be filed toward the edge of my desk when I notice Claire trying to sneak out the door before I can catch her. "File that, will you, Goodnite?"

"No?" she responds.

"It's an order. Since you seem to be so bored on desk duty."

"Fuck," she mumbles under her breath as she grabs the files off my desk and heads out into the station, making me bite back a smile. If I know anything about my sister, it's that if she sees my reaction, she will seek revenge. We both know she's not going to do that paperwork but find trouble instead. My sister is a nut, and I love her so much.

I catch a look at Wes and notice his mood has dropped significantly since his wife left the room. It instantly sobers my own mood and makes the smile I was trying to hide only seconds ago slide right off my face. I know it could be weird that my best friend married my sister, but I love them both, and honestly, it's the best thing that could have happened to either of them. I'm so happy for them, even if I'm also secretly a little jealous.

"So, Palmer?" I ask after I clear my throat.

"Yeah," is all my friend says, letting me know the case that took him out of state was, in fact, because a former teammate of ours, Sam Biggs, who we lovingly referred to as Palmer—since he got caught jacking it in the desert—had ended his own life.

PTSD is the dirty word that no one talks about, but every former service member has firsthand knowledge on some level. If you would have asked me out of all our former teammates, who would be the one I would worry about most, it wouldn't have been Palmer. The kid was happy-go-lucky, he never let shit get to him, and he always kept us in stitches.

But I guess he had monsters of his own that he kept on a much deeper level than any of us realized.

"Fuck," I say without even realizing the expletive

escaped my lips. I rest my elbows on my desk and let my head fall into my hands while I give my feelings over my fallen friend a moment to sink in.

"Yeah."

"We should have known something was wrong," I admit my greatest failure. It's hard to hold so much guilt. I've failed so many people who deserved better than what they got from me. Claire, Anna, Emma, and now Palmer. Who's going to be next? It makes the dark thoughts I try to keep buried so deep rise to the surface. Maybe I should throw in the towel too.

"We should have known," he repeats my words, and I look up to see his green eyes stare hard at me. "But it's not your fault."

"I know that," I lie.

"Do you?" he asks me, still seeing more than I think I care for.

"Of course," I tell him before changing the subject. "So how are Chancey and Monk?"

"They're having a rough time of their own."

"I see Jake has some opposition in Washington. I wasn't sure there was anyone alive who didn't love the golden boy." I smile. "It's good for him though."

"Rick had a rough moment, but it all worked out," Wes says.

"How so?" I ask, suddenly worried about two of my oldest friends.

"Someone kidnapped his daughter, but we got her

back," he admits. "Off the books."

"And everyone is all right now?"

"The aide-de-camp took a bullet, but he's fine." Wes shrugs.

"I read he got hurt in a hunting accident."

"Sure." He shrugs again.

"Wes—" I start, but in typical Wes fashion, he hones in on what I don't want to talk about.

"So I heard you and Emma got along well at the crime scene last night," he interrupts, dropping a bomb on my desk like it's not a big deal. Asshole.

"Sure," I mirror his earlier evasions.

"So how did that go?"

"It went."

"Come on." He laughs. "You have to give me something."

"I don't have to give you shit, you asshole." I laugh.

"I have been telling Claire to leave you both alone for months, even though everyone in the tri-state area knows you guys banged like bunnies for weeks right after my wedding," he says. "I have to admit, I even thought that baby was yours when she said she was pregnant."

"Yeah, me too," I murmur quietly as my heart pangs. I don't think I've ever wanted someone to be pregnant more in my entire life. For a hot second, my greedy mind thought that if that baby was mine, I could have her forever. Fucked up, I know.

"Hey, I'm sorry," he says, realizing how much the whole thing hurts me. "I had no idea."

"What?" I laugh again, but there's no humor behind it. "That I'm in love with her and she doesn't love me?"

"I don't think she doesn't love you," Wes replies. "I just think it's…"

"What? Complicated?"

"Yeah."

"Because that's exactly what Emma said every time I brought up the idea of our being together," I confess.

"Ouch."

"Yeah."

"Maybe you just need to move on," he suggests. "Find someone new."

"And how did that work out for you?" I ask, because we both know that the years in between when he fell in love with Claire and when they finally got their shit together, he was almost completely unbearable to be around. Wes was angry, moody, and had a death wish. All of which made him a great SEAL and then FBI agent. But who he was then and who he is now are night and day.

"You love her that much?"

"Yeah."

"Then quit fucking around," he says. "Lay down

the law and go get your girl."

"And how did that work out for you?" I ask again raising an eyebrow because we both know that hindsight was more than twenty twenty for him where my sister was concerned. "Because I remember Claire jumping out bathroom windows and hot-wiring cars to get away from you."

"Yeah." He smiles a ridiculously dopey smile. "But it was fun to chase her for a bit."

"Yeah, all right." I roll my eyes.

"No," he says, looking like he's really thinking about it. "Maybe that's exactly what you need to do. Maybe you need to chase her a bit. Knock her off balance and see what she does."

"You're ridiculous," I tell him.

"If by ridiculous you mean ridiculously happy, because I finally have the girl I wanted my entire life and I get to go home to her every night. And every night, I get to hold her in my arms and watch her lose her temper over something stupid and then fuck the frown right off her face, then yeah, I'm ridiculous."

"That's my baby sister you're talking about," I warn him.

"And you already got your free punch in when I slept with her the first time," he throws right back. "Now she's my wife and you are over it."

"This is true."

"Now tell me I'm wrong," he says as he makes his

way to the door of my office. "I dare you."

"I really hate you."

"No, you don't." He laughs as the door closes behind him, and I think maybe he's not completely wrong. Maybe I need to knock Emma off balance a little bit. Maybe I need to show her that I'm done fucking around. I'm all in. I mean, what's the worst that could happen?

Famous last words, right?

five

like a bad penny

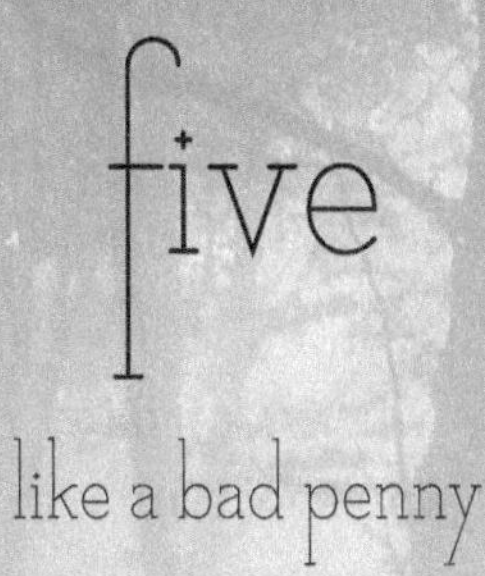

I let out a frustrated sigh as I pull my car over to the side of the quiet suburban street and park. After Wes left my office in search of his wayward wife, I grabbed my jacket and headed out. It was time I spoke to Ashley Horner's family.

This is by far the shittiest part of the job. I like to think this is a small drop in the bucket of things I have to atone for in my life, and one day, hopefully before I die, I'll know I've made up for all the bad I have done and all the damage I caused.

Then again, maybe not.

I unfold my long legs from the driver seat and shut the door behind me, beeping the locks as I go. The guys in the station would have a field day if I got my duty vehicle stolen on a next of kin notification. Those loveable bastards would eat me alive at the first smell of blood in the water.

I tuck my keys in my front pocket and make my way up the slender walkway to the narrow house with white clapboard siding. The Horner's live just outside George Washington Township, which is probably why I hadn't recognized their names. GWT is a pretty small town, and more often than not, it feels even smaller, but I had never seen Ashley before in my life.

My fist falls heavy on the door as I knock. I don't have to wait long when it swings open, revealing a tired-looking woman in her mid to late forties. Her brows pull together in a way that hints that she frowns often and rarely smiles.

"Can I help you?" she asks when she gets a good look at my badge.

"Are you Mrs. Horner?"

"Yes," she says hesitantly. "What do you want?"

"I'm Captain Liam Goodnite with the George Washington Township Police Department," I inform her. "May I come inside?"

She sighs but pushes the door open for me to follow her into the small sunroom where an older floral sofa sits faded in the middle of the room. Other than being sparse, the home is clean and nice.

"Gary!" she shouts. "Get in here."

"What now, Evelyn?" a man, late-forties to early-fifties and slightly overweight, asks as he makes his way into the room.

"I don't know," she says in a nasty tone. "But I'm

sure it has something to do with Ashley. It always does."

"That girl is like a bad penny," Mr. Horner agrees. "She's always turning up where she isn't wanted. What kind of trouble has she gotten herself into now?"

"Maybe you both should have a seat," I suggest gently.

"Better just get it over with," he says. "We prefer to rip the Band-Aid off where she's concerned."

"If you're sure?" I ask.

"I am," he says, pulling his wife into his arms. "She's nothing but bad news."

When I ran Ashley's background this morning, I didn't find anything that suggested she was the bad seed her parents seemed to think she was. She had a decent job making a low wage, her apartment was clean, and even her high school transcript was decent. I'm not sure what they found so appalling, but I was going to find out, because no matter how they felt about her, she didn't deserve to die like that.

"As I told your wife, I'm Captain Liam Goodnite with the George Washington Township Police Department, and I regret to inform you that your daughter, Ashley Horner, was found dead last night."

I wait for them to respond. To ask how or why she died. To inquire after their missing grandchild, cry, yell—I don't know, *something*. But when it became abundantly clear they were going to have no reaction at all, I buried my own personal feelings about these people and got down to doing my job. Whether they were responsible or not, I was going to find out who did this to Ashley if it was the last thing I did.

"When was the last time you saw your daughter?"

"When she told us she was pregnant," Mrs. Horner says after a minute.

"Were you excited about the baby?" I asked, figuring they were absolutely not, but I had to ask anyway.

"Of course not," she scoffs. "She was throwing her life away."

"How so?"

"She was offered a modeling contract," she answers. "She was going to get out of here and live a great life, and instead, she got pregnant and started waiting tables. How could we be happy about that?"

I didn't answer her. My opinion isn't needed, she was clearly on a roll all on her own.

"And the baby's father?" I ask. "How did he feel about it?"

"Who knows?" she answers. "We never met him. He didn't even have the decency to do the right thing."

"And what would that be?"

"Marry her? Make her get rid of it? I don't know! Something!" she shouts. "She was throwing her whole life away, and it was embarrassing!"

"What was embarrassing about it?"

"Everyone was talking," she says. "I couldn't go to

the market or church without people whispering about my daughter. She humiliated me! I begged her to get rid of it, and she said no! Can you believe that? I told her she wasn't welcome back here unless she gave it up for adoption. Something. But to clean up her act."

I mean, who needs enemies when you have parents like this? It makes me thankful for my loud, overbearing, annoying, but totally amazing family. I would be lost without them. All of them.

"And you never saw her again?" I asked.

"No."

"Did you ever go to her apartment on Ashland?"

"No," Mr. Horner finally speaks up. "We had no idea she even moved to GWT."

"That's all I need for now," I tell them as I grab a business card out of my wallet. "If you think of anything else, give me a call."

I leave the Horners to their misery and jump in my car. I wipe a frustrated hand down my face before I stab the key in the ignition, jerking the gear shift into drive and heading back to the station. My phone buzzes in my pocket, and I pull it out and slide my finger across the glass to unlock it.

Emma: Autopsy is done.

There it is. I equal parts love being around Emma and I hate it. But I will swallow all the heartache she needs to dish out to me, because it's the least I can do. Whatever she needs to make her okay, I'll do it. So I respond, letting my fingers fly over the keys while I'm stopped at a red light.

Me: I'm on my way now.

Emma: See you soon. ;)

I love the station. It's my home away from home. Actually, I spend significantly more of my time there than I do at my actual house. My career is everything I have. I guess now is when I could wax poetic about how I could have everything I ever wanted if I wasn't such a fucking idiot, but my dad always says you can't put the toothpaste back in the tube, so we need to make the best of it. Which is why I'm heading back to the place that usually makes me the happiest, even though today it makes my gut burn, because instead of the world open in front of me, I have an autopsy meeting with the one woman who drives me crazy and makes me regret everything I ever did in my life except her. I'll never regret her.

I drive back to GWT, not seeing the town I've loved my whole life. Instead, it's like a cloud hangs over my head. I need to figure out how to right the ship that is my life, and fast, before I sink for good.

I turn into the station and drive around back, pulling into my parking spot by the glass front door that opens to the hallway where my private office is. With a heavy sigh, I push open my door and step down from the Tahoe, slamming the door closed a little more forcefully than I meant to. With a final look back at my car and a sad and pathetic shake of my head, I pull open the glass door and head inside, only not to the safety of my office but down the stairs to the basement where Emma Parker, one of the best medical examiners I have ever seen work, is waiting to tell me how Ashley Horner met her end.

I take a deep breath and try to steel my emotions. If I can just lock everything down, I might just get through this briefing. And then I push the heavy steel fire door open, and I'm stopped in my tracks by the most beautiful smile I have ever seen.

"Hey, Lee," Emma greets me before pulling her surgical mask back up over her mouth and nose.

"Hi, Em," I say and have to clear my throat. So much for getting through this meeting in one piece. "What do you have for me?"

"A lot was the same as the girls last week," she explains as she snaps on a new pair of latex gloves. "Ashley Horner, nineteen, died due to complications from a crude cesarean section."

"Official cause of death?" I ask her.

"Exsanguination," she says softly. "The incision site was never closed, and she bled out on the floor."

"That's consistent with the crime scene."

"Yes," Emma agrees thoughtfully. "It is."

"Any blunt force trauma?" I ask. "Or do you have anything as to how they got her like this?"

"Yes." Emma turns the body so I can see a small

puncture mark on the side of her thigh. "Ashley was injected with a sedative."

"So are we looking for a medical professional?" I wonder what kind of doctor would cut up pregnant girls like this.

"No, I don't think so," she answers. Her brows scrunch up over her eyes, and I can see she's working through a puzzle. "The downward trajectory of the needle is more consistent with someone administering an EpiPen, a quick strike like a snakebite. Hard and fast."

My eyes snap up to hers the minute the words are out of her mouth, and I watch the skin of her neck and ears flush a pretty pink. I know if she weren't wearing that damn mask, I'd see she's blushing all over, and I love it. Maybe she is still affected by me. That does more to boost my mood than anything else could have.

"Emma—" I start, but she interrupts me.

"Just forget I said anything at all." She rushes to get the words out quickly while she covers Ashley Horner back up and shoves her back in the drawer. "It was a Freudian slip."

"I think it was on purpose," I say, my voice lower than before as I move toward her. She's too busy flitting about the room like a hummingbird to notice my movements.

"I'll run some toxicology tests on Ms. Horner and on the Jane Doe from last week and see if I can find anything," she explains without looking at me as she snaps her gloves off, but by then it's too late. I'm right beside her.

"Stop, honey," I say softly. I don't touch her, but I lean in as close as she'll let me before she gets that wild look in her eyes.

"Lee—" she starts.

"Stop," I repeat just as gently as before. "It's time to stop running."

"No," she whispers.

"I'm done fucking around."

"You're w-what?" Emma stammers, and her ears turn red, a clear indicator she's no longer scared but pissed as hell. Good. I don't want her meek and mild; I want my tiger back.

"I'm done fucking around," I say once more. "You are mine, and I am yours."

"You know why we can't be together," she whispers harshly.

"I know why you think we don't deserve to be together," I respond. "And honey, we did wrong by Anna, but it's also time for Anna to be given her fair share of the responsibility for what happened. We can't keep living our lives like this."

"I'm with someone else." I can see she's scrambling. Emma is trying to throw up roadblocks left and right to discourage what has been happening between us all along, but it only serves to make me even more determined.

"Then end it."

"You can't be serious," she snaps.

"I'm as serious as a heart attack," I say as calmly as she is agitated. "You can't honestly admit he gives you anything close to what I can."

"Conceited much?"

"Am I wrong?"

"You're an asshole, Lee."

"I'm an asshole who's been in love with you for a long time, and now I'm done fucking around."

"So you say," she snarls. "I'm having someone else's baby, Lee."

"I see that," I tell her. "But what you clearly do not get, so I'm going to spell it out for you, is that I don't care whose baby that is. His, mine, someone else's, the minute I claim you for good, I claim that baby too. I'll give it my name and raise it as my own with you in our home."

"Lee—" she starts, but I don't give her a chance to run.

"I will teach it to catch a ball and ride a bike, and I will walk the halls with it in the middle of the night. I'll do it all with a smile on my face, because I love you that much. So I'll love it too."

"Stop calling her 'it.' She's a girl," she says softly.

"Then I'm going to cry like a fucking baby at all the dance recitals," I tell her honestly. "But I'm still going to teach her to throw a ball and ride a bike. So

I'll let you have your space—for now—but think on what I've said."

And then I place a hard but quick kiss on her lips and head back up the stairs to my office, where all the paperwork I know my sister did not do is waiting for me. Thankfully, no one is in the back hallway, so no one sees me with the enormous erection my standoff with Emma has left me with.

I quickly shut the door behind me, make my way around my desk, and sit down in my chair. I need to cool my thoughts, which are decidedly on the wrong track for the middle of a workday. But I can't stop thinking about the way her big blue eyes went soft when I said I didn't care who the biological father of the baby is. And the way her blonde-and-pink curls were barely contained on top of her head in a disaster of a bun. I love the way her little bump is barely concealed under her tee and scrub bottoms, and the little noises she makes when her breath hitches ever so slightly drives me wild. Everything about her has my dick painfully hard in my slacks, but I have to go slow with Emma. I swear to God that I won't scare her away.

And then there's a knock at my door.

six

"**C**ome in," I bark and hope to hell and back that my desk hides my dick that is refusing to listen to reason and play by the rules.

The doorknob slowly turns, and it seems like an eternity before my door pushes open the tiniest bit, and the person on the other side is the last person on earth I thought would seek me out right now. I figured I pushed her too far this afternoon, but now, I'm not so sure.

Emma slips through the partial opening of the door and closes it softly behind her before turning around to face me, but she still doesn't give me her eyes. She leans against the heavy door as if she's using her tiny body to block my path. On her face, she wears an expression with a wild air and a little desperation. Her eyes are closed tight.

"What can I do for you, Emma?"

And then she opens her eyes, and those baby-blues burn me where I sit. But still, she looks nervous, like she doesn't know how to ask for what she wants. And color me surprised.

"I-I-I—" she stammers.

"You what, honey?" I ask softly, and fuck if I don't hope she asks me for me.

"I need…." she whispers, and I can see the pink flush on her cheeks and down her neck, where I'm sure that pretty blush stains the tops of her full breasts as well.

"I know what you need," I respond, and her eyes flair. "Come here, Emma, but lock the door first."

Her mouth opens and she pants a little. She looks around wildly, and I'm not sure if she's going to come to me or run. Then, after seeming to come to a decision, she turns around, and I think, *Now, I've really pushed her too far.* And I wonder how long it's going to take me to make up the ground that I've just lost by jumping the gun. But she surprises me, and maybe herself a little too, when she flips the fucking lock and takes a step away from the door.

I hold my breath as she moves another nervous step toward me, and then another, and another. I let her come to me, when what I want to do is jump up and pull her into my arms. But I've made myself clear. The ball is in her court now, and she has to come to me on her own terms. We'll figure the rest out from there. But

I know one thing for sure—after this, there will be no going back.

I push my chair back a bit to make room for her to stand between me and my desk. Emma rests her ass against the edge of the scarred wood and wraps her delicate fingers around the edge on either side of her.

"I need you," she whispers before leaning down and pressing her mouth to mine.

I deepen the kiss, and she lets me take over. I run my hands up and down her sides, warming them with the heat of her body. Over her arms, her little belly, and then up to her breasts. She gasps against my mouth when I find one of her nipples, and I soothe it with the back of my knuckles before trailing my hands down the middle of her belly to the tie at the front of her scrub pants.

I untie the knot and let them gape open then slide my hand down the front and into her panties. She widens her stance to let me in, and I feel how wet she is for me on my fingertips. I toy and tease, letting my fingers circle her pussy but never dipping inside. She rocks her hips against my hand, but I don't give her what she wants, not yet anyway.

And then I pull my hand free, and Emma lets out a little whimper, but it doesn't last long when I grab the waist of both her scrubs and her cute little cotton panties and slide them down her legs. She kicks out of them and her black-and-white-checkered Vans sneakers, and I help her up onto my desk, where she leans her weight back on her elbows.

"Lee," she whispers, and I smile for what feels like the first time in forever as I toss the end of my tie over my shoulder and spread her creamy thighs with my hands.

Every muscle in her body contracts when I place a soft open-mouthed kiss on the very center of her, and she drops down to lie on her back on my desk when I lick her. Her legs threaten to close over my ears, and I hold them tight as I suck her clit into my mouth before starting the circuit all over again.

Her whole body shakes and quivers, and she lets out soft little pants. She fists my hair in her hands and pulls me tight against her pussy, and I'm all too happy to follow. And then as I roll my tongue over her one last time. She lets go, and it's as beautiful as it is life-altering.

"Lee," she whispers. "Please."

I stand up over her and unbuckle my leather belt. I unzip my slacks and have to hold my cock tight in my fist when I look at all her flushed, creamy skin down to her glistening pink pussy.

I notch the very tip of me against her opening and slowly sink inside. I clench my eyes tight, and she wraps her legs around my waist, encouraging me to move. I lean over her and rest my hands on either side of her head before taking her mouth in a savage kiss. She blossoms under me, taking everything I have to give and more.

And then I pull my hips back, sliding almost all the

way out, and drive back in, making her gasp again. I do it again and again, loving the soft sounds she makes when she gives herself over to the pleasure between us.

Emma wraps her arms around my waist, and I feel her grip the back of my shirt in her fingers. I wish we were skin-on-skin, but this will have to do for now. Tonight, I'll make sure there is nothing between us, and then I'll take my time and savor the moment.

She bites down on my bottom lip, and the sting drives me hard. I plunge deep, faster and faster, until she drops her head back on the desk and opens her mouth. I crush my lips to hers and thrust my tongue inside as I swallow her cries, and her body grips me tight as she comes.

I drive deep twice more before planting myself inside her and following her over the edge. I drop my forehead down to rest on top of hers and listen to our breaths saw in and out of our chests. For the first time in a long time, I feel settled. A rightness of the world blankets me as all the pieces click into place, and one thing I know with absolute certainty is that Emma is mine.

She pushes gently on my shoulders before whispering, "You're crushing me."

I place a soft kiss on her lips and stand up, letting our bodies slide apart. I tuck myself back in my slacks and do up the front. I see she's trying to come to terms with what just happened, but I'm not going to give her the opening to run again. I can't do it. But I will be gentle, so I sit back in my chair, grab her pants and panties from the floor, and slide them up her legs one at a time before tying the drawstring gently.

I hold a hand out to her to help her sit up when I see her flopping around a bit like a roly-poly. Her belly is just big enough to be cumbersome and keep her from sitting up on her own. She takes my hand and lets me help her, which is a victory I'm happy to claim.

"Lee—" she starts with a worried look on her face, but I don't let her finish.

"No, Emma," I tell her gently. "This happened. We are happening."

"Maybe this was a mistake," she says, and I can tell she's grasping at straws again because she's scared, but I'm done. No more running unless it's to each other.

"You know this wasn't a mistake."

"I don't know anything," she snaps as she slides her feet back into her sneakers and pulls her Van Halen T-shirt down over her belly.

I'm just about to reply, when there's another knock at the door.

seven

do you know what you're doing?

"This isn't over," I warn her as she makes her way over to the door.

"It is," she replies as she flips the lock open, making me roll my eyes.

"I was serious when I said—"

"I know, you're 'done fucking around,'" she says with finger quotes, which if anyone else did them, it would drive me insane.

"It's true," I remind her. "You're mine."

"We'll see," she says as she pulls open the door, giving my meddlesome but loveable sister entrance.

Yes, we will.

"Where have you been?" she snaps as she looks between us.

Claire can't find anything wrong, even though she's a damn good detective and I know it. When she knocked on the door, it was all I could do to calm Emma down as I had just slid her panties and scrub pants up her legs and tied the drawstring in a neat little bow. I would have loved to have had more time with Emma to talk about what had just happened but it looks as if my luck hasn't changed much.

But when I tucked myself back in my pants and buckled my belt, everything changed. Emma used those precious moments to re-erect the walls she previously held between us. So now she's in a fluster to get out of my office and put some much-needed distance between us. And I'd give her that play—for now.

But as I watch her, I can't help but think maybe Wes was right after all. Maybe Emma nees a push. So she can run, but I'm going to chase her, because this is right. I've never felt surer of anything in my life, and I'm done feeling guilty and fighting it.

"Well?" Claire snaps.

"I was here," I answer. She shoots me a hard look, and I know she's watching me for any inconsistencies, but there are none. What's happening between Emma and me is none of her business, at least not yet.

"Dispatch is trying to page you," she says quickly. "There was another body."

"Fuck," I bite out. I should not have fucked Emma in my office, but I will not regret it, because whether she knows it or not, she gave me the opening I have been waiting months for.

"I should go prep the Body Mover for transport,"

she says quietly—too quietly.

"Em—" I start, but she's already out the door. I stand up to go after her, but Claire stops me.

"Let her go," she commands me gently.

"Don't," I warn my only living sister. We had grown up, just Claire and me, but after we learned of a half-sister no one knew about after she was murdered, I realized that life was too short and that I had to make the most of it. But that doesn't mean I'm going to let Claire walk all over me now. That doesn't mean she won't try, but it's who we are.

"Do you know what you're doing with her?" The way Claire looks at me says she doesn't exactly trust me with her only friend. And she has a point. I'm not the hero in this story. But I'm also not going to let her discourage me for going after what I want. What I need.

"Yes," I answer honestly, looking her in the eyes so she knows how serious I take these words. "I'm making her mine."

"But at what cost, Lee?"

"I love her."

Her face softens. "Then go get your girl."

"Christ. Pregnancy has made you soft," I tease her.

"If you think I'm bad, you should see Wes," she says with a mischievous smile. "He cries at the drop of a hat these days."

"I know. He's a regular water pot."

"Love you," she murmurs softly, wrapping her

arms around my middle.

"Love you too, sis."

eight

"Try not to burn the building down," I say, rolling my eyes at my sister. She just flips me off. The move makes me smile.

She really is the very best sister, and I love her. I can't even think of what my life would be like if she was taken from our family forever, either when she was a little kid or last year. It's hard enough knowing we had an older sister we'll never know because she was murdered by a serial killer. Thankfully, we get to have her three children in our lives, even if Eric is away in the army, and Brooklyn is away at school. Seth is in the loving care of my parents, and we try to all be there for him.

What I want to do is go after Emma. I don't do that. Instead, I chase my sister out of my office, taking the written dispatch note from her, and head down the hall toward the back entrance to the station. I push out the glass door and take a deep breath before jumping in my car.

I turn the keys in the ignition and tip my head side to side to crack my neck. I need to get my head back in the game. Whoever is waiting for me at the next crime scene deserves my total attention. So I use the time as I drive through town.

The address I was given takes me out into the suburbs, where my sister and Wes live. It's a nice neighborhood, the kind only a lot of money can buy. I'm surprised by the surroundings as I see the blue-and-red lights flash in front of a decent-sized home. Until now, our previous two victims were young, single pregnant women. They had no family, no partners, and no money. So part of me thinks whoever is waiting is not connected to the baby snatcher case.

I pull my keys from the ignition and step down from my Tahoe, shutting the door behind me. I beep the locks on my key fob and drop them in my pocket before making my way up the three-car driveway.

"Hey, Cap," Jones greets me in the front of the house.

"Hey, Jones. What do we have?" I ask him as I take the paper booties and latex gloves he has in his hands for me. Fuck, more blood. "Thanks."

"We got another one," he says sadly, and I look at him—really look at him. Jones and his wife, Linda, have been trying to have a baby for a while now to no avail. Last I heard, they were considering adoption, but it's so expensive, and a cop's salary does not allow for that.

"How are you doing?"

"I'm okay," he answers. "I just can't for the life of me figure out why someone would be stealing babies."

"That's what we're going to find out, buddy," I remind him.

"I hope so."

I follow him into the house, and we don't have to travel far, because the victim is lying in a huge puddle of blood on her living room carpet. Fuck. Not again. Between Claire and Emma both being pregnant, I've become really sensitive to this. It burns deep that someone could do this to women. But I use that burn to drive me to keep going. I have to find out what happened to these people. They deserve that justice.

"Weird," Jones mumbles as he watches the scene. I can tell that, like me, he's taking in every little detail. If ever there were a cop who worked harder to make detective, I never knew them. He has a sharp mind and a great gut intuition. So, looking at him, I can tell that something other than the gruesome picture painted in vivid detail before us is eating away at him. I just don't know if he knows what it is yet.

"It's more than weird," I reply, even though I'm pretty sure he was just thinking out loud. "Something on your mind, brother?"

"The living room," he answers me, and he's still whispering, and that in and of itself has the hairs on the back of my neck standing on end.

"What about the living room?"

"Every one of these girls was cut up on the living room floor," he replies. "Why here?"

He's right. Every last victim, of which we now have three, was hacked to pieces on their living room floors, their babies stolen from their wombs, and left to bleed out and die all alone. But why?

"You think they were entertaining?" I ask.

"I think they all knew the same person," he says. "Because I can't think of one person who would cut out a woman's baby and leave her to bleed like that, let alone three."

"Amen."

"Well thanks for the invitation to the party," Emma chirps as she rolls into the room in her coveralls and plastic booties. "But we really gotta stop meeting like this."

"Amen to that too," I mumble, and Jones just nods.

"I'm going to go look around the house," he says. "See what else stands out."

"You got it."

I don't look at him as he walks out of the room, so I definitely miss that he left it with a smirk playing out on his face and a wink to Emma's assistant, Maryann. I just keep my eyes on Emma as she tends to the latest victim.

"Come here, boss," she says as she waves her hand

at me, and I move to squat down where she's doing her preliminary work before she moves the body to her morgue. "Look at this."

"What am I looking at?" I ask as I stare at a small purple bruise.

"Another puncture mark," she answers. "I found one on the original victim too, and I'm running another toxicology report on her as well. But at this point, I think it's safe to say—"

"Don't do it," I warn.

"—that you have yourself a serial killer," she finishes, and I let my head drop back to examine the ceiling.

"I really, really fucking hate when you say that," I tell her as I stand up and look at her. She smiles brightly in a sweetness-and-sunshine way that both steals the breath from my lungs and scares the ever-loving shit out of me.

"I know."

"Hey, Em?" I begin, but she interrupts me, her voice soft and low and shoots straight to my heart.

"Not yet, Lee."

"We need to talk, honey," I say just as softly, matching my tone to hers.

"I know," she replies. Emma glances away for a moment before looking back, her blue eyes burning into my violet ones. "But not yet, Lee. I need to get this body to the morgue."

"Okay."

I stand back and watch as she jumps in the driver seat of the van that is ridiculous with her metal-band stickers all over the back. I know the minute she turns the key in the ignition, because Drowning Pool starts blaring "Bodies" at an inhumane decibel. And then she peels out of the parking lot, and I watch her head out into the night and away from me, but I do it for the first time in a long time with a small amount of hope burning like the last ember in a campfire through my chest.

nine

home alone tonight

This is not how I saw my night going.

But still, I have hope. Tonight, Emma didn't shut me down; she didn't lash out like she normally does when I push for more. I told her we needed to talk, and she said she knew. That wasn't her professing her undying love for me, but I'll take it. I know I have to prove to her the kind of man I can be. I have to earn her trust, and I haven't done that yet, but I'm going to do it now. So, no, she didn't jump in with both feet, but she also didn't tell me to go to hell.

As soon as I walked in the front door, I locked up my gun and stripped down before pulling on a T-shirt and a pair of gray sweatpants. I made my way back downstairs to the kitchen and pulled a beer out of the fridge, popping the top. I tossed the bottle cap in the trash, tipped the cool glass to my lips, and drank before setting it down on the island.

It's been a shit day.

There's something that's bothering me about these victims. Who would cut up expectant mothers like that and why? It's just not something I can wrap my mind around, and I hate it. When I think of these women and what they went through before they died, I can't help but think of Emma and Claire, who are also expecting. The idea that someone would want to do either of them harm makes me sick to my stomach.

I grip the edge of the countertop in my hands, my knuckles turn white under the pressure, and I hang my head forward. I squeeze my eyes closed tight and try to force the images from my brain, but it's no use. Tonight, the ghosts don't want to let me go.

I get as good a hold on my emotions as I can. I pull in a deep breath through my nose and force it out from my mouth. I suck in another and hold it for as long as I can before I push it out then do it again and again until I feel like my heart isn't going to explode out of my chest.

And then I pull my phone from the pocket of my sweatpants and slide my finger across the glass to unlock it, and I dial my favorite pizza place in the neighborhood. I order my favorite pie with everything on it and hang up. I place my phone on the stone countertop and finish my beer before tossing it in the trash and grabbing another from the fridge.

I look around at the home I remodeled from the old heap it was when I moved in. I had no idea what I was doing at the time; all I knew was I needed to do something with my hands. I needed to sweat out the demons that were dogging my every step, and I needed to do something that got me out of my own head. What I didn't know then but do as I look around now—and I can't help but come to terms with—is that everything I did to fix up this house, and also myself, was for her.

The doorbell rings, and I nab the cash I pulled from my wallet earlier from my pocket and make my way back to the front of the house. I look through the small, beveled glass window in the door and see the kid that usually brings me my pizza. You can never be too careful, and when you're in my line of work, that factoid is glaringly obvious.

"Hey, Joey," I say when I pull open the door.

"Hey, Mr. Goodnite. Here's your pizza," he greets, handing me the hot box. I have it on good authority that Joey is saving his money to help his mom out before he goes into the navy. And knowing my nephew did the same to help his mom before he left for the army makes me think twice about Joey and send him on his way with a little extra.

"Here you go," I tell him, handing him the wad of cash. "Keep the change."

"Thanks!" he replies enthusiastically, making me smile. I watch him head down the walkway to his car before I close the door and send the bolt home, locking me in for the night with my own ghosts.

I carry the steaming cardboard box into the den and drop it down on the coffee table before heading back into the kitchen to grab the beer I opened. I don't bother with plates or cutlery, but I do grab some paper towels off the roll on my way through and get ready to settle in for another night home alone.

I collapse on the old leather sofa that has been all over the place with me and in every apartment I've ever lived in on my own. I didn't have the heart to part with it when I moved into this house and filled it with new furniture, but it was perfect for a small room that opens off the kitchen, where I have a warm rug on the floor, a stone fireplace, and a large television. The only thing this room is missing is a dog, but my schedule barely has enough time for me to keep myself alive, let alone a dog. Maybe I should get a cat. I could be a guy with a cat.

I pop the lid on the pizza box and pull a big piece out, folding it like a taco and diving in. I pick up the remote with my free hand and flip through the channels while I eat way more pizza than I should. I can't remember when the last time I ate today was though, so it all balances out.

I just missed the end of the game, not that my heart was in it anyway, and the local news isn't going to say anything I want to hear right now. I've avoided it as much as I can, and because one of the victims was from outside of GWP, the crime beat anchor has been blowing up my phone line for a couple days now. I know, at this point, it's only a matter of time.

I let out a sigh and shut the TV off. I gather up my trash and take it into the kitchen, stuffing it in the trash bag. I tie it up and take it out through the washroom and into the garage where I keep my trashcans.

When I come back inside, I make sure all the doors are locked, turn off all the lights, and head upstairs to try to get some sleep.

I pull back the covers on my bed and climb in. I toss and turn for an hour at least, and my last thought before sleep finally claims me is that I really should get a cat. If I had a cat to come home to, maybe I wouldn't feel so overwhelmingly lonely. Because not once tonight did Emma call me.

I'm running.

Wes and I were sitting in his office while I was trying to get him to pull his head out of his ass where my sister was concerned, when his phone rang. "Yeah," he said when he picked up and hit the speaker button as soon as he realized something was wrong. "Anna's at the church. She says she knows who the killer is," Claire panted, her breathing harsh.

"Lee's here. We're on our way," Wes said to Claire just before he hung up. I was already standing by the time he finished the call, and we were both running out of his office.

I parked closer, so we jump in my department vehicle and take off. Claire is probably the farthest out, with Wes and me closest to the church. As we drive, I pray that I get there in time and so fucking angry that Anna would try to solve this herself. This killer is dangerous. But she is so sure she could show my dumb fucking ass that she's an equal

I should have known she would do something like this. I should have made things clearer with her. Told her straight out that I was head-over-heels for Emma and that there was no hope for her and me.

She couldn't see that, somewhere along the way, while she was falling in love with me, I was falling for Emma. Or she didn't want to see it. I don't know. This is just a big fucking mess. I pull into the parking lot of the church and bare-ly have the Tahoe in park before I'm running for the church doors with the car door hanging open. I spot Claire heading for the church from the other end of the lot. Somehow, she made it here before us. We are all in hot pursuit, but nothing would prepare us for what we'd encounter when we enter the sanctuary.

I'm running as fast as I can, pushing my body as hard as it will go. From the minute Wes hung up the phone after talking to Claire, I knew Anna was going to do something stupid. I could feel it in the pit of my stomach. How could she? The answer is simple—she wants to belong that badly, to be worthy of someone like me, whether I'm in love with her or not.

As I run up the steps, I pull my sidearm from its holster and steady my arms. I breathe in three times and out one to center my focus. I push open the big double door and enter the sanctuary. I draw my side-arm when I hear Anna's scream.

Nothing could prepare me for what I was about to see.

"What have you done?" I hear the man scream from the side, but I can't look at him now.

"Police!" Claire shouts. Emma is right beside her as they barrel into the room. "Don't move!

But the man does with a maniacal look on his face. There's a wildness that sparks behind his eyes. One that I've seen before in the men we fought overseas, the fanatics I've encountered back home.

The knife arcs through the air and plunges into Anna's heart, her body glitters with the blood already spilled from previous stab wounds. Until the day I die, I will never forget the look of panic, of desperation, on her face as it changed into resignation. She knows she's going to die.

And then Claire pulls the trigger over and over again. I watch as she empties her magazine into the man's body until he falls limp to the side. "No!" she screams, but Wes grabs her from behind to stop her from closing the gap between her and the bloody body on the altar of my family church, while I race up the steps to get to Anna.

I push the man's body to the side while Emma rushes in from the back, drops to her knees by Anna's side, and unties her hands. Blood covers them both. "Anna! Goddammit, stay with me!" Emma shrieks as she tries to stop the blood flowing so freely from slices and holes places all over her petite body. Claire drops to her knees beside me.

"What can I do? Tell me what to do!"

"Just stop the bleeding."

"Emma," Anna rasps. There's a rattling behind her voice, and everyone in this room knows what that means. A death rattle.

"Save your energy, babe," Emma tells her sweetly.

"I see it now," she says. "It was wrong of me to want him. He was always yours."

"No," Emma denies as the tears stream down her beautiful face. "Don't say that."

"Love him for me," she begs, and my breath seizes in my lungs as my own tears burn behind my eyes. After everything we've been through, she's stepping aside in our twisted love triangle, only now there are just the two of us who will be left standing.

"No. You do it, because I won't!" Emma sobs.

"He loves you," Anna rattles.

"I don't care," Emma lies.

"He's going to... to need someone to... to love him."

I can see it's taking all her energy to get her last wishes out, and I hate it. She's dying, because of me. Because I didn't love her. Someone should have loved her.

"No, Anna," Emma pleads. "Anything but that."

"Just... love him." And then her eyes dip closed, never to open again as the last of her breath wheezes out of her body.

"Anna!" Emma cries.

"Emma, honey," I say as she clings to her.

"No!" she screams as she pulls away from me. "Don't touch me!"

"Emma," Claire calls out, looking unsure of what to do.

"No, Lee. This is all your fault."

I feel as if she slapped me.

"Emma, you can't mean that," I plead.

"She wanted so badly to belong to you, to fit into your world, and that pushed her straight to this moment," Emma accuses with an eerie coldness in her voice.

"Emma—"

"Do me a favor, Lee, and just stay the fuck away from me." And then she storms outside.

Wes grabs Claire from behind again and pulls her away from Anna, while I just sit there feeling numb. How could everything go to shit in the blink of an eye?

"Let me go!" she wails. Her voice is harsh and raw.

I look away from them and back to where Anna's lifeless body is lying still on the altar steps, but when I do, it's not Anna's dark eyes that are open with nothing but emptiness behind them, all the life to live sapped out. It's the cool blue of Emma's.

I gasp as I come awake. Sitting up quickly with my knees bent, I try to catch my breath, but it's no use. I can't shake the image of Emma on the altar. I can't lose her now that I've just gotten her.

The room spins, and with a steady hand out to brace against the wall if I stumble, I race into the bathroom. I don't bother to flip on the lights. I just drop to my knees and empty the contents of my stomach, wishing I hadn't overindulged on my favorite comfort food of pizza and beer.

I flush the toilet and stand up on shaky legs as I make my way to the sink. I splash cool water all over my face and rinse out my mouth before I make my way back to bed and lie down, all the while hoping I can find peace enough to sleep, but the grips of the dream still hold me. All I can do is pray the nightmares don't find their way to the living, because I know without a doubt I couldn't survive that.

ten

uncomfortable

"**G**oodnite," I answer the phone on my desk when it rings. I've been sitting here for who knows how long, staring at the case files, and wondering where the connection lies. I just can't figure it out, and it's bugging the shit out of me, because I know it's there.

After struggling to get back to sleep in the wee hours of the morning, I tossed and turned, tangled in my sheets with sweat coating my body and visions of Emma's lifeless eyes haunting my thoughts. So when sleep finally came, it wasn't a deep restfulness. I just fell into a void of nothing. When I woke up again, I felt like shit, and I still do, but when my alarm rang, for the first time in a long time, I felt like something was happening. I hopped in the shower and dressed quickly. I skipped breakfast, knowing I would eat when I had another chance, but I couldn't ignore the feeling in my gut that something would break loose today.

I just know it.

So when I got to the station, I made a quick cup of coffee in the kitchenette off the bullpen before heading to my office. My goal for today was simple—pour over these case notes and pictures until something shakes loose. Fortunately, I didn't have to wait too long, because when my desk phone rang, I picked it up without thought and answered.

"I figured it out!" Emma says, the excitement in her find ringing clear in her voice.

"What?" I love the sound of her voice no matter what, but when Emma is on the hunt, there is a confidence in her tone that is sexy as hell. Her mind is brilliant, and I love to watch her puzzle something out.

"Come down to the lab and see."

"I'll be there in twenty," I reply. The eagerness bubbles up from my belly. Could this really be the break in the case we need? Fuck, I hope so.

"See you then," she says before ending the call.

I flip through the case photos one more time so they are fresh in my mind. I'm sure there's something I'm missing, and if I just keep it all fresh, eventually the pieces will fall into place. I tip my mug back and chug what's left of my now cold coffee, letting the bitter flavor flow over my tongue and give me something to focus on. Sometimes, a quick change of direction will also help my brain find the connections, but still, there's nothing.

So I set my mug down on top of my desk and close

the file. I leave my office and take the stairs down to Emma's basement lair so I don't have to wait for the elevator, but when I get there, I see she's not alone. I decided to give her a minute to finish up her business with this mystery woman I've never seen before in my life, but I can't help but overhear their uncomfortable exchange.

"Just… think about my offer."

"Yeah," Emma says, and I don't like the tone of her voice. Something sounds… I don't know… off with her, and I don't like it.

I peer through the small rectangular window in the heavy utilitarian-gray door at the woman. She's well dressed, older but not too old, probably in her late-fifties to early-sixties, and maybe a little posh even. Her dark hair is pulled up on top of her head, and she's wearing an expensive suit; that much I know.

I can also tell she's giving the hard sell to Emma. I just don't know about what yet. Whatever it is, she looks uncomfortable, and I don't like that at all. So I knock on the small window, startling both women. I wait a beat, letting them get their bearings before I twist the doorknob and push the heavy metal door open.

Both Emma and the mystery woman turn to me, and I don't know what it is about her. I can't say what it is, because I do not know her, but there's something about Emma's posture with this woman that bothers me. It sets my teeth on edge.

"Excuse me," I say once I've fully entered the

room, letting the heavy door close behind me. "I'm sorry to interrupt."

One look around the room and we all know my words don't ring true. And while Emma's face is wreathed in relief, the other woman's is covered in annoyance and frustration. I can't say I'm sorry for either.

"Well, if you'll excuse us," Emma says softly, and I hate that it's not her usual confident self shining through. Whatever this woman did to strip her of that, I hate, and I hate her for it. "I have to get back to work."

"Yes, of course," the woman says, pasting a fake smile on her face. "But don't forget what we discussed. Make the right decision, because we both know that's not you."

And with those last words, she flows out of the room. Emma and I stand there and watch her go. My curiosity is piqued by the woman who could ruffle Emma's hard-won confidence, and not in a good way.

"Who was that?"

"Madame Driskill," she answers like I should know who that is.

I feel my face pull into a frown, but it's one more of confusion that anything else. "I don't understand."

"She runs a high-end private adoption agency out of the city," Emma explains.

"You're giving the baby up?" I ask as something dark and heavy slithers into my belly. Even though her baby is not mine, I have spent plenty of time imagining my life with both of them in it. The idea one of them won't be there hurts.

"No," she says with a heavy look of her own. "Of course not."

And while I feel a sudden relief at her words, I can't help but to ask, "Then why was she here?"

"Jerrod set up the appointment," she answers, and her distaste in the answer is palpable.

"Why?" I question softly. I want to reach out to her, to hold her when she looks this distraught, but I also know she would not welcome that right now.

"He said he wants to be with me, but only if I come without my baby," she answers. "He's been pushing the issue lately."

I want to punch his freaking face in. What kind of guy wants the girl but not the baby he helped make? This Jerrod guy is an absolute tool.

"Emma—" I start, but she won't let me finish.

"No," she says, effectively cutting me off. "It's fine. Well, it's not fine, but it is what it is."

"What are you going to do?"

"Not Jerrod," she mumbles, and my heart feels lighter than ever, and I decide that, for her, I can change the subject. As much as I want to push her to pick me, I don't want to push too hard too fast. So I decide to bide my time and wait. And hope she's ending things with the tool.

"So you found something?"

Her face instantly brightens. "Yes!" she says excitedly again. Her whole demeanor changes before my eyes as she brushes off the unfortunate meeting with the adoption lady. "I did. Come on over."

I follow Emma deeper into the lab, where she grabs a stack of photos and pins them to the big board in her office. I can see they are zoomed-in pictures of puncture marks on several different bodies.

"You remember how I showed you the puncture mark on the thigh of Ashley Horner?" she asks me.

"I do," I reply. I fold my arms across my chest and settle in, because if Emma says she found a link, she undoubtedly did, and it's going to be huge.

"Well, I found puncture marks on every victim." She smiles broadly, and I love watching her revel in her discoveries.

"That's great," I tell her. "Any idea what they were injected with?"

"Yes! I was lucky and found trace amounts of the substance in the majority of the victims that we can make the leap that that's what was used to incapacitate them before they were operated on and left for dead."

Her excitement is rolling off her in waves, and I can't help but feel it too. "What is it?"

"Atropine," she answers immediately.

"I don't know what that is," I admit.

"It's a medication that can be used to treat a host of symptoms, including colds, asthma, intestinal issues, eye problems, and heart conditions. And it is available both over the counter and by prescription in tablets, inhalants, injectables, and eye drops."

"And you think the victims were injected with this?" I ask.

"I don't think it; I know it," she answers. Her confidence shines through once again, and I say a silent prayer of thanks.

"What would happen if they were injected with it? I know you said it's prescribed that way, so it can't be too bad."

"It's not if given in the correct amounts. But if overdosed, atropine becomes a poison that takes effect very quickly. They might experience a rise in body temp, dry mouth, sometimes muscle spasms, and then total paralysis with some cognition. But they might also have blurred vision and/or hallucinations, since it's derived from belladonna."

"So they may or may not have been cognizant while they were cut open and then died?" I feel anger rising up inside me at the thought of someone doing that to another person.

"Let's just hope they weren't," she answers me softly. I clench my fists at my side and feel her touch my arm where the muscles are bunched tight. "We won't ever know. And honey? You can't carry that with you."

"I know," I reply, my voice tight, and I need to brush off this heavy blow so I can find the bastard who would bring these women so low.

"I didn't bring you down here to upset you," she says, and she surprises me by wrapping her arms around my middle in a hug. I close my arms around her, holding her to me and accepting the comfort she's offering.

"I know you didn't."

"I just wanted to help."

"You are," I tell her as I hold her tighter. I breathe in the scent of her hair and let the heaviness go before I explain. "It's hard for me to see these women like this and not think of you and Claire. If I'm unable to protect either of you—" I can't get the rest of the words out.

"You will," she says quickly. "I know you will."

Her words are like a balm for my soul. And I can't help but feel that if Emma believes in me, I might just be able to believe in myself. So much so that the next words that tumble out of my mouth fall free before I have a chance to sensor my emotions.

"Have dinner with me." But I also won't regret them, because even if it's moving faster than she wants, I just want to be near her.

"Okay," she says softly, her words muffled by my chest, but I still hear them all the same. And I feel on top of the world again, because Emma said yes.

eleven

be with me

"**A**re you ready to go?" I ask Emma after I knock on the door to her basement lair. I have my jacket over my arm, and I jingle my change in my pants pocket to hide my nerves. I've known and worked with Emma for years, and we've been friends just as long, but now that I know how high the stakes are, I can't help but be nervous. Like a teenage boy asking my crush to the prom.

"Yeah," she says softly, and as she looks at me, her face gentles. Honestly, I could have just watched her close up shop for hours as she sorted paperwork and filed whatever was on her desk from the day. She's that damn beautiful. But the way she looks at me now renders me speechless.

She neatly stacks the last of her papers in a pile before dropping them in her desk drawer and locking it with a key. There's something about seeing this organized and orderly side of Emma, who is more than a little wild, that I can't help but smile at.

She scoops up her purse and jacket and walks toward me. I take her jacket and hold it out for her to slide into, and she does so, tugging her long hair out as she goes.

"Thank you."

"Of course," I say with a smile. "What do you feel like?"

"Honestly?" she asks almost hesitantly.

"Yeah," I reply. "I'll take you wherever you want to go."

"Okay, but it's silly," Emma warns.

"There is nothing too silly. Seriously, whatever you want."

"It's weird," she explains, "but lately I've had the worst heartburn, and the only things that put out the fire is the chili from Wendy's and a double cheeseburger even though square patties are scary."

"That *stops* your heartburn?" I can't help the broad grin that spreads across my face.

"I told you it was weird."

"It's not weird. Okay, it is, but only that it cures your heartburn. So let's go."

"All right."

I place the palm of my hand at the small of her back, and I feel her heat on my skin as I lead her out of the building and to my car. I beep the locks on the key fob and pull the passenger door open for her. Before she can get a foot on the running board, I place my hands on her waist and lift her up into the cab. She lets out an undignified squeak, and it's singlehandedly the most adorable sound I've ever heard.

"All set?" I ask, and when she nods, I shut the door before rounding the hood and climbing in the driver seat.

"So…." she trails off.

"Yeah?" I prompt, turning to look at her. "How was your day?"

"Better. I feel like everything is just about to break through."

"It will," she assures quietly. I hate that she's so quiet and not her usual loud, confident self. "I know you'll figure it out."

"Thanks." I smile at her when we stop at a light. She doesn't know it, but her words of encouragement go a long way to help me feel like I can do it. "So… dine-in or takeout?"

"Don't laugh," she hedges.

"I would never," I swear to her with my hand over my heart.

"I would love to get takeout and watch TV," she says sheepishly. "My feet are killing me."

"I'm so sorry," I tell her instantly. "I had no idea."

"I know." She smiles. "That's why I'm telling you."

I pull into the Wendy's parking lot and around to the drive-thru. When I reach the speaker, Emma orders just about one of everything on the menu, making me smile. She laughs a happy sound when I tell the kid taking our order to double it, because for the most part it sounded good, and if I found her eating leftover tacos in the morning for breakfast, then that wouldn't be a bad thing.

"So… my place or yours?"

She looks at me with all of her trust laid bare for me to see before she answers me, and it isn't until right now that I realize my heart's beating in my throat. "Yours."

"Roger that."

I pay the kid at the window and collect an insane amount of paper sacks and our drinks, placing the bags on the floor in the back and the drinks in the cupholders. She unwraps the paper from her straw and sticks it through her lid before doing the same with mine.

"Thanks."

"Of course," she replies with my earlier response to her, and when I glance at her, her wide blue eyes are full of… hope.

I pull into my driveway a minute or two later and park. I jump down from the driver side and hurry around the hood. Emma is just reaching for the drinks in the center console when I pull open her door and pluck her from her seat.

"Lee!" she gasps as I set her on her feet.

"What?" I open the back door and grab the bags full of junk food.

"I'm not light, and now I'm even less so," she explains. "You gotta stop doing that."

"One," I respond as I tap the tip of her nose with my index finger, "you are not heavy, and two, even if you were, I would not make you jump up or down from this high of a vehicle. It could be dangerous."

I can't decipher the meaning behind the look she gives me, but I do know it was a good one when she whispers, "Okay, Lee."

I lead her up the walkway to the front door, even though she knows her way around from our time together before. This is a new beginning; we're both trying to find the right footing this time, and I know I hope we can go all the way.

I unlock the front door and let us in, turning on the lights as I go. I move all the way into the house and set our dinner on the coffee table in the den. Emma places our drinks down and dances from foot to foot nervously.

"Come on," I tell her as I grab her hand and drag her back through the living room and up the stairs to my bedroom at the back of the house.

"Lee...." she drawls, her voice filled with apprehension.

"This isn't that, honey," I tell her gently. "At least not yet. But I'm telling you now that when you open that door for us, I'm there, and I'm all in."

I push open my door and immediately move to the wide dresser that sits low against the far wall of the room. I pull open the drawers and close them quickly, knowing exactly where each item I want is. I make two stacks of clothing before handing one to Emma.

"Here," I tell her as I place a pair of soft plaid flannel pajama pants and one of my T-shirts in her hands. On top of the stack is a balled-up pair of socks.

"What's all this?" she asks, her blue eyes wide.

"You've had a long day on your feet," I answer. "Now it's time to get comfy, so you can settle in and take over the remote to my television while we eat way too much junk food, and then I'm going to rub your feet. And then, when you're ready, I'm going to take you home. Okay?"

"Okay."

"I'm going to change too, but I'll do it in the bathroom down the hall," I say, hitching my thumb over my shoulder in the general direction of the door to the room.

"Okay," she says again, and whatever passes behind those big blue eyes is so good and so beautiful it almost drops me to my knees.

"I'll meet you downstairs," I tell her as I grab my stack and make my way down the hall.

I change into my gray sweatpants and a plain white T-shirt before jogging down the stairs two at a time. Having Emma under my roof does something to me. There's an extra pep in my step and a lightness in my soul, but overall, it just feels right.

I start sorting food from the bags into two equal piles on the table and for the first time realize just how much we ordered. These quantities rival any amount Claire could and would take down. While I try and maintain a fairly healthy diet, because forty is *not* the new twenty, my sister's taste in food is atrocious.

But what my girl craves, my girl gets, so I'm putting my mostly good eating habits to the side for the night. I've just finished divvying up our dinner when she walks into the room, looking like every man's wet dream. My pajama pants are too big, even with her belly, and too long, so she has them cinched at the waist and the cuffs rolled up to reveal my wool socks. My T-shirt, which was so long on her she didn't need the pants, hangs off one shoulder. She has her messy curls twisted up on top of her head and dark-framed glasses on her face.

"I had to take my contacts out," she explains with a wave of her hand in front of her face.

"No problem," I tell her with a smile. "Have a seat."

She curls up in the corner of the large sofa and grabs a chicken sandwich and some barbecue sauce from the table before she opens it up and starts changing it exactly how she wants it.

"It's good, I swear," she says when she catches me watching her.

"I don't doubt it," I agree as I lift my own sandwich

to my mouth.

"Want to try it?" she asks as she holds hers up in front of mouth, and the move is so intimate and speaks of trust and a closeness between two people that I've only ever dreamed about with her that I couldn't say no, even if I wanted to.

"Yes," I whisper hoarsely before I wrap my hand around hers and slowly take a bite of her sandwich. The gasp that slips from her lips has my heart racing and the blood in my veins headed south.

"It's good, right?" She smiles.

"Yeah."

"Here," she adds, handing me a packet of barbeque sauce for my own sandwich. "I'll even share my magic sauce with you."

I hold my breath, because I know for a fact that Emma did not mean that to come out as dirty as it did. And that is obvious when her eyes widen and she rushes to clear up the situation, making us both laugh.

"I did not mean it that way."

"I know." I grin, handing her the remote. "Do your worst."

She takes it from my hand with a wicked gleam in her eyes that I want to fall into over and over again and starts flipping through the channels before she settles on *The Real Housewives*. I can't help the chuckle that escapes my mouth.

"Don't laugh!" she cries. "I love these bitches.

They're so crazy."

"I'm not laughing," I tell her, but I'm smiling. I'm sitting here in my living room, wearing sweats and eating fast food, but I'm doing all of that with her, and it's the time of my life. It's beautiful.

After a while, she wipes her hands on a napkin before she starts packing up the leftovers, which there are surprisingly few of, and carries them into the kitchen while I gather up the trash. I'm just standing up when she comes back in, and when my eyes meet hers, she looks surprised.

"Jesus," she says before I can ask her what's wrong or if it's the baby. "Those should be illegal."

"What?" I ask.

"Those sweatpants and that bulge," she says, making me laugh. "It should be illegal to look like that. It's like porn that slaps you in the face with a monster dick. Put it away."

"I'd love to." I laugh. "But your staring at it is not helping."

"I know, you're right," she says, licking her lips. "But I can't stop."

"Emma, honey—" I start, because I don't want to rush into things with her. I want this thing between us to go the distance and go strong, and even though I had her on my desk just days ago, I know that that won't happen if I fuck her every chance I get. I need to show Emma that I want more from her than a quick fuck, I want everything.

"No," she says as she places her slim fingers over my mouth, and my arms go around her. "I know what you're going to say. We need to slow down; we shouldn't rush things. But here's the thing, Lee."

"Yeah," I mumble around her fingers.

"I want you," she says, her eyes burning into mine. "I'm choosing you."

"Emma…?" I ask, afraid to let the rest of my burning question be spoken into the air.

"The door is open, Lee, and it's going to stay open." And then she slides her hand from covering my mouth to the side of my neck, and she presses up on her toes, because she's tall but I'm still taller, to touch her mouth to mine. And my whole world narrows down to just her and me.

I tighten my arms around her and deepen the kiss, licking into her mouth. She gasps against my lips when she rocks her hips against me and feels my hard length pressed up against her, ripping a low rumble of a groan from deep in my chest. Instead of stopping, she wraps her long legs around my waist so my cock presses exactly where she wants it. I pull back to catch my breath and watch her shiny blue eyes to see if she really wants this like I want her—like I want all of her.

"Take me to bed, Lee," she says confidently, and I do just that.

I walk with her wrapped around my waist, her round belly keeping her from pressing against me fully, but she holds on tight to my shoulders as I take the stairs back up to my bedroom. I hold her hips tight to mine with a hand on her ass, and I use the other to pull back the covers. Laying her down in the middle of the pillows, I sit back on my knees between her legs.

I lean forward and place a kiss on the corner of her mouth before I sit back and gently take the glasses from her face. Folding them carefully, I place them on top of the nightstand. I gather the hem of her borrowed shirt in my hands and pull it up inch by inch until she leans forward and lets me slip it over her head. I pluck at the clasp of her bra that rests between her full breasts and watch them spill out when the cups part. I help her shrug out of the straps and push the delicate material aside, not bothering to watch as it falls to the floor, because I can't take my eyes off of her. She's that fucking beautiful. She was gorgeous before, but now, as her body changes, she's magnificent. I could say she would be even prettier if it was my child, but that's a lie. If she's serious, if Emma really gives us this shot, that child is mine no matter whose DNA runs in her veins.

I kiss my way down her neck and over the tip of one breast. The little gasp that slips from her lips when I flick the tip of my tongue over the stiff peak turns me on even more. And when I suck deep, rolling the tip under my tongue, she grips the short strands of my hair in her fingers and rocks her covered pussy against my hard cock.

"Lee," she moans as she pulls my hair and rubs her hot center over my length again and again. Even with clothing between us, I can tell she's wet underneath it all.

"So sensitive," I mumble as I nip and lick my way over to her other breast. "Could you come like this?"

"Lee," she pleads as she rocks against me, her movements faster and more frantic than before. "Please."

"I want to give you that," I tell her just before I lick her tip one more time. "I want to watch you come undone on my tongue and then my cock."

"Yes," she pants as she rocks against me, making me groan. If I'm not careful, this will end before it begins.

I lean forward again, this time bracing my weight on my forearms, one on either side of her shoulders. I suck her neglected tip into my mouth and roll it under my tongue, this time as I rock my hips against hers.

"Yes," she whispers as her nails bite into my scalp. "Yes, yes, I—" And then she tips her head back, her back bowing off the bed as she lets go, and it's glorious.

I keep my hips pressed hard to hers as she comes back down to earth, and I let her nipple go with a pop before sitting back on my heels and pulling my own T-shirt over my head. Her dazed baby-blues watch me with a hunger that has lust singing in my veins. I love that she wants me as much as I want her, that her hunger and passion rival my own. If ever there was a woman who was a perfect match for me, it's Emma.

I don't rush as I pull on the drawstring of the pajama pants she's wearing, even though she clearly wants me to hurry. This is like unwrapping the best present under the tree on Christmas morning. I don't want to rush; *I want to savor.*

I tuck my fingers into the waistband of the pajamas and her panties and lower them down her legs. She shimmies her hips to help get rid of them before parting her creamy thighs again, and I was right; she's fucking drenched, and the lips of her pussy glisten with it.

"Lee," she says. "Hurry."

I push my sweats and my boxer briefs down my thighs. My cock springs free, and I grip it tight in my fist to keep from coming. I lean over and grab a condom from the nightstand drawer. We didn't use one in my office, but we should have. I haven't been with anyone else, but she obviously has, and there is nothing wrong with that, yet we should still be smart about it. So I grab one and rip it open without asking, rolling the latex down my hard length as quickly as possible.

I place my hands on her inner thighs that are spread open like a butterfly's wings and lean in as I notch the tip of my cock against her opening. I press deeper against her and slowly slide all the way in. Emma sucks in a breath through her clenched teeth, and I'm not far off either.

I glide in and out of her at a slow pace, the angle deep enough that she rolls her bottom lip in her mouth and bites down. I enjoy the feel of her grip on my body, but it's not enough. And while it feels good, we both know how great it can be when she comes on my cock.

She grips the sheets tight in her hands when I roll my thumb over her clit as I pump into her waiting heat. I circle in time and watch her gorgeous face as she fights it. She doesn't want to come yet, but she can't stop it. Together, Emma and I are like a runaway train.

"Not yet," she pants, but she's so close she can't stop, and I don't want her to.

"Yes," I growl. I flick her clit and drive a little deeper, a little harder. The mewl she lets out drives me even rougher.

"Lee," she cries. "I can't stop. Don't stop."

"I won't, baby," I tell her, and I couldn't if I tried. "Fuck, fuck. I need it."

"Lee."

I push down on her clit, and she detonates around me. Her back bows and her breath catches, and she clamps down on my cock so hard I think I might have seen stars. I place my hand back on her thigh and hold her open to me as I drive into her hard, over and over again. I ride through her orgasm and feel that tingle shiver up my spine. I plunge deep one more time before she pulls me over the edge.

I drop my forehead to her chest. Our breaths saw in and out of our lungs while we both come down, and when I look up at her, her face is so beautiful and open; she's hiding nothing from me. There's a lot of lust and the look of a well-fucked woman, but there's also a fair amount of hope... and love.

"Be with me," I whisper. I said I was done fucking around, but I also don't want to send her screaming from my house. This right here and all the nights to come. And the mornings and the daytime and all the in-betweens until the day they put me in the ground. I want those with her and only her.

"I'm with you," she whispers.

"Yeah?" I ask, unsure if she really means what I want it to.

"Yeah," Emma agrees. "I'm in love with you, Lee."

"Now I want to fuck you," I tell her, making her giggle.

"Umm… I think you just did that."

"But now I want to do it and hear you say it again, and I can say it too, because, honey, you have to know I do. But instead, I have to get up and get rid of this condom," I explain, and she's still giggling, but it's the brilliant smile on her face that has starbursts in my chest, because after all the pain I gave her, I've finally given the woman something of beauty, when she has deserved nothing less the entire time.

"Okay," she says with another smile.

"But then when I come back to bed, we can make out like teenagers," I tell her. "Because I'm forty, not twenty."

"Okay."

"And then you can ride my hand until you come,"

I say, making the smile slide right off her face and her pupils flare. Oh yeah, my girl likes that idea.

"Okay," she whispers harshly.

"And then you can tell me that you love me again when I fuck you. Does that sound good?"

"Yeah," she says softly, and her eyes have that hazy look.

"Now kiss me," I order.

"Okay."

I touch my mouth to hers. And then I slide out and make my way to the bathroom to get rid of the condom. I walk back into my room, and she's sitting up on the bed. She has the sheets pooled over her lap, hiding her center from me, but her lush breasts, which are fuller with pregnancy, hang in front of her, and my cock twitches.

"What?" she asks when she catches me staring.

"I wish I was a painter," I tell her. "So I could picture you like this forever. You deserve to be painted."

"Lee," she says, pushing up onto her knees when I sit on the bed. She does not hesitate to come to me. Wrapping her arms around my shoulders, she pulls me to her.

I kiss her. We're all mouths and lips, kissing and tasting while we touch. I lose myself in her like never before. Together, we're both comforting and familiar and also brand-new and exciting.

I roll her to her side and wrap myself around her

back. She tips her head back so she can kiss me again, and I let my hands skim over her breasts and pinch her nipples. She moans when I do, and the sexy sound goes straight to my cock.

She wiggles her ass against my crotch, and I know the minute she recognizes her effect on me as I skate my hand down her belly to between her legs.

"I thought you said you weren't twenty anymore," she gasps when I stroke down one side of her hood and then up the other.

"Apparently, with you, I am."

She grabs my hand between her legs and plunges my fingers into her pussy while she rocks against the heel of my hand. And fuck me if the sight of her fucking herself on my hand, taking charge of her pleasure and what she wants, what she needs, doesn't have my cock harder than ever.

"My girl wants to come," I mumble against her bare shoulder where I touch my lips to her in a gentle kiss.

"Yes," she pants. "I want you to make me come."

"Anything for you," I say as I smile against her skin. She tastes salty and sweet.

I add a second finger and plunge them deep, curling them against the spot inside her that I know for a fact drives her crazy. I pull them out and circle her clit, spreading her moisture all over her. I dip my fingers inside her again and again, making her squirm, and then up against the side of her clit again.

"Please," she gasps so sweetly that I push her outside leg up in front of her and slide in deep from behind.

I wrap my arms around her, and she holds onto my forearms as we rock against each other. She feels so tight this way. And this way we can lay skin-to-skin, when we can't while we're face-to-face right now. I kiss the side of her neck and nip at her ear while out bodies slip and slide against each other.

Her breast is full and heavy in my palm, and I roll it under my fingertips as her pussy works my cock. She tips her head back on my shoulder so that her mouth can touch mine. She opens under me, and I do not hesitate to lick inside, letting her tongue tangle with mine, and she meets me thrust for thrust. Where earlier was frantic and wild and explosive, this is a gentle coming together where we know the other won't run away at any moment. Emma and I have finally given in to the pull between us for good.

"I love you, Lee," she says, and then she just lets go, and it is so beautiful I couldn't hold back if I tried. Not my words, not my orgasm, so I give both to her. Only to her.

"I love you too, Emma," I reply, and then holding her tight in my arms, I follow her over the edge. We stay like that for a long time, and then finally, she rolls in my arms and settles where she was always meant to be. We shut off the lights and fall asleep, together.

twelve

gone to shit

"**O**h fuck no," Emma groans and pulls a pillow over her head when my alarm goes off. The fact that she is the world's worst morning person makes me smile.

"Go back to sleep, honey," I tell her. "You have time before you have to get up. I'm going down to the basement to get a workout in."

"Yeah, no," she mumbles already half asleep. "Don't put me down for cardio."

"No, honey. I won't."

I tuck the covers tightly around her body and throw on a pair of shorts and my running shoes, and I jog down to my basement gym to get a good workout in. I run on the treadmill but find myself eager to get back to my girl upstairs in my bed. I push myself to finish my workout with pull-ups and sit-ups, and then I run back up the stairs all the way to my bedroom to find Emma exactly where I left her—curled up under my pillow. Her gorgeous ass is peeking out at me from under the covers.

"Emma," I whisper. "It's time to wake up."

"Argh," is all that I get from under the blankets, so I make my way into the bathroom and flip the shower on so the water warms up. I strip down and toss my workout shorts in the hamper before heading back to the bedroom.

I slide the blankets back so she's uncovered except for her head, which is still under the pillow. I glide my hand down her spine before slipping over her hip and down her thigh.

"Emma, it's time to wake up."

"No," she growls, and it's both adorable and terrifying.

I decide should she turn a little violent to not have my favorite body parts so close to her, so I stand up and move away from the bed, backing toward the bathroom before calling over my shoulder, "If you get up right now, I just might have time to fuck you quick in the shower."

Emma pops up out of the bed, looking adorable with her wild eyes and disaster of hair that's sticking up in every direction. I think I even see a little bit of drool at the corner of her mouth, and I love it. I love everything about Emma waking up to me in my house.

"It's the hormones," she says as she parades her naked ass past me and heads into the shower. "It has nothing to do with you."

"Of course not," I reply with a ridiculous smile stretching my face.

"I wouldn't want you to get an overinflated ego," she tells me.

"Me neither," I agree, not even pretending to be serious about it at all.

"It's because of the pregnancy hormones that I'm going to let you fuck me in the shower and then not utter a peep while I eat cold Wendy's fries for breakfast."

"Of course."

"Not a peep!" she shouts, and I just nod as she steps into the large shower stall. "Now get in here and fuck me so we can get on with our day."

And I do exactly that. Which is why when I walk into my office two hours later, I do it with a smile on my face and an extra pep in my step.

Today is going to be a great fucking day.

Beth Andersen was a corporate ad executive for a huge marketing company headquartered in Manhattan, which is how I found myself spending the day driving into the city with Jones so we could go interview her colleagues.

I had just poured myself a cup of coffee when Jones popped his head into the little kitchenette to let me know he called the offices and that there was someone available to speak to us today. The owner and CEO had been dodging my calls for a few days now, so I wasn't going to be unavailable when he finally was. I was bothered by the fact that he was avoiding a police interview, but not enough to have my Spidey senses tingling. There were enough bodies piling up that I had a feeling this guy wasn't the killer, but he was still guilty of something. Probably tax evasion. I should have Wes look into him.

Jones and I pulled up at ten to ten and marched into the offices with smiles on our faces and our badges clipped to our hips. We were sent up to the twentieth floor to meet Beth's personal assistant, Emmory.

Emmory is young and beautiful. She has long red hair and flawless skin. I would put her in her early to mid-twenties, probably a recent college graduate. She's wearing office-style clothes that are just a little shy of the mark. Her skirt is short and tight, and her button-up blouse appears to be missing more than a few of the buttons at the top.

But it was the way her entire demeanor changed when the CEO walked by her to his office that got my attention. She preened and presented like a happy peacock to get his attention.

"So what can you tell us about your employer?" I ask when I can't take another minute of her fidgeting in her seat.

"Probably not much. I hadn't worked for her for long."

"Did she get along with other employees?" Jones asks.

"No." She laughs. "Beth was a total bitch."

"So you didn't get along with her?" I ask.

"She was a hard woman to work for," she answers, looking nervous as she glances between Jones and me. "I'm not in trouble, am I?"

"No," I say with my most charming smile.

"Was she involved with anyone here at work?" Jones questions.

A strange look passes across her face that tells me there is definitely something going on here. "Not to my knowledge."

"And do you know who the father of her baby was?" I ask.

"No, no one knows."

"How long have you been fucking the boss?" Jones probes, making her jump.

"I… uhh… I don't know what you're talking about," she stammers.

"And how long had Beth been sleeping with him before that?" I test.

"Beth was a cold bitch who couldn't make anyone love her," she snaps. "But I have no knowledge about her personal relationships."

"Thank you, Emmory," I say gently. "We'll see our way into Mr. Preston's office now."

Jones and I both stand and walk across the room to where the big glass-fronted office has its entrance. I knock on the door out of courtesy before pushing it open and walking in.

"My next appointment is here, honey," Preston says into his phone. Which is fascinating, because he's not talking to Emmory. "I have to go."

"What can I do for you, officers?" he prompts after he hangs up the phone, placing it in the cradle on his desk.

"We wanted to talk to you about Beth Andersen," I reply. "We're with the George Washington Township Police Department."

"It's just awful what happened to her," he says, but his tone suggests that he couldn't care less. It sounds to me like Mr. Preston wove a pretty tangled web.

"It is," Jones agrees. "How long had Beth been working here?"

"About a decade," he answers. "She came to us right after she graduated from NYU."

"Was she a good worker?" I ask. "Did she get along well with the other employees?"

"Oh yes," he says with a smile on his face, obviously relaxing in his confidence. I smile back. "She worked very hard, climbed the corporate ladder, if you will, rather quickly. And everyone around her loved her."

Interesting, because that's not what Emmory said.

Now, she could just not have liked Beth, because she was a rival for Preston's affections.

"And when did Beth tell you that you were the father of her baby?" I ask.

"Who told you?" he roars, sitting up in his chair, his relaxed expression morphing into one of outrage.

"You just did," Jones replies.

"You don't understand," he hurries to explain. "Beth and I had an understanding."

"And what did your understanding entail?" Jones asks, looking like he wants to throw up.

"On nights that we worked late, we were together," he says with a shrug. "It was simple."

"When did it become *not* simple?" Jones presses.

"When she found out she was pregnant," he spits out. "I told her she needed to get rid of it. I even offered to pay for it, and she said no. Can you believe it?"

"And what happened then?" Jones ignores him.

"She moved to New Jersey," he says, like living anywhere past Soho is disgusting. "She started talking about being a family, and I had to put a stop to it. I'm married. We weren't ever going to be a family."

"And what did she do when you spelled it out for her?" I ask.

"She was upset, obviously, but we talked about it, and I think she finally saw reason," he replies.

"And what was that?"

"I hooked her up with La Famille Agency," he explains.

"What's that?" Jones asks.

"It's a premiere adoption agency," Preston says, looking proud. "Madame Driskill only gives babies to the most exclusive families. The children are cared for in every possible way, and she compensates the biological families significantly. It was perfect."

"So she was going to sell you baby?" Jones clarifies. "And you were fine with that."

"It's not like that," he says with a sneer. "You don't understand."

"Then explain it to us," I say quietly.

"My wife is barren," Preston explains. "She wants to adopt."

"So you were going to take your mistress's baby and give it to her," I say, and now I'm the one who feels sick.

"Yes, but now that baby is gone and my wife is going to have to wait for another," he grumbles, sounding more like a spoiled child. But what he does not sound like is a murderer.

"Well," I say, standing up with Jones following my lead. "Thank you for your time."

We climb into the car and start heading back to GWP.

"I feel dirty now," Jones says.

"Yeah." And that's all we say the whole ride back

to the station.

I park around the back, and we walk in through the glass door, both waving our badges over the pad as we go. I need to see Emma. Something about the exchange with Preston has left me feeling unsettled, and I take the steps down to the basement two at a time after I part ways with Jones.

But voices inside her office stop me with a hand to the door before I push it open.

"Do you need to be here?" a man snaps.

"Oh, I really do," my sister replies with her usual amount of sass. "But the question is, do you?"

"Call off your guard dog, Em," he snaps.

"No," she says firmly, but I can hear her voice shake with nerves. "Whatever you want to say to me, you can say in front of my friend."

"Do you really think he's the guy?" he snarls.

"Yes."

"That he's ready to play daddy now?"

"I don't think that it's any of your concern," Emma says quietly.

"Madame Driskill said you turned down her offer," he snaps. "Are you crazy?"

"Maybe," she says. "But I'm keeping my baby."

"Then you lose me."

"I already did," she replies.

"Don't say I didn't warn you." And then he moves

to leave. I quickly back up around the corner, so it looks like I'm coming around the hall from the elevator when he shoves through the door.

There's something about this guy that just rubs me the wrong way. Why would he be pressuring Emma to give up their child? What kind of man does that? I just don't get it. I'm sure I'm missing some piece of the puzzle, but truthfully, I don't care, and I don't want to know. His loss is my gain. I lost Emma once, and I won't do it again.

He comes barreling around the corner, and I lean into him at the last second, feigning surprise. I pat him hard on the back of the shoulder after we collide, and when I do, I notice a hair on the back of his collar. I gently pluck it from his back as carefully and quickly as possible without him noticing.

"Sorry, man," I say to him good-naturedly, when really I just want to punch him in the face. "I didn't see you coming."

"Do yourself a favor and run far and wide from that one," he says to me, gesturing over his shoulder. "She's nothing but bad news."

"I'll take that under advisement."

I watch him head down the hall and climb in the elevator. When the doors close behind him, I decided to head back to my office and put the hair in an evidence tube. I don't know why; I just do what my gut is telling me to. Besides, I know that Emma will be fine with Claire.

Everything will be fine.

Little did I know it had all gone to shit. I just didn't know how yet.

thirteen

"Hey," Emma says when she sees me standing in the doorway, watching her. There's a gentle smile on her face that tells me that she's happy to see me.

"Hey, yourself," I reply. "Are you ready to go?"

"Yeah," she says as she once again stacks her paperwork and tucks them in her desk drawer before locking it and tucking the key in her purse.

"I have one last thing," I say hesitantly before handing her the vial with the hair in it.

"What's this?" she asks, and I do something I promised I would never do again. I lie to Emma. I just hope it doesn't come back and bite me in the ass later.

"I don't know," I tell her. "It was recovered from some of the stuff at one of the crime scenes. If you could run it, I would appreciate it."

"Sure thing," she says with a smile, and I feel like an asshole for deceiving her. "I'm happy to help."

"Thanks."

"Ready to go, big man?" she asks me.

"Yeah," I tell her. "I thought we could go back home for dinner."

"We can't," she says sadly. "I ate all the leftover fries for breakfast."

"I thought I'd cook, brat." I laugh.

"I don't even understand the words that are coming out of your mouth right now," she says. "What is cooking?"

"Funny, funny," I reply as we push out the door and head to my car.

"I know." She fake-flips her hair back, making me laugh.

I beep the locks and pull open the passenger door for her before wrapping my hands around her waist and lifting her up into the cab. I make my way around the front of the Tahoe and climb in the driver seat before heading home with my girl.

I hold her slim hand in mine on my thigh as I drive through town. Pulling into the parking lot of her apartment complex, I shut the car down.

"I thought we were going to your house?" she asks me, her face awash with confusion.

"We are." I smile gently at her. "But you don't have any shit there. And honey, I want your fruity shampoo in my shower and your pregnancy vitamins in the cabinet. I want whatever comes with you, because I just want you, in my house, in my bed, in my life. It's just that simple."

"You want me every day?" she questions hesitantly. "Just you and me?"

"Until the baby comes along and makes three," I say, giving her honesty, because that's what she wants and what I want her to have from me—at least as much as I can give her when I can. "I just want you."

"Okay, Lee."

"And, baby?"

"Yeah?" she asks.

"Pack a lot, because this place is a dump and you won't be coming back," I tell her as I jump down from the driver seat and walk around the hood to her door. Like I suspected she would be, she's spitting mad when I pull open her door.

"I already said okay, Lee," she snaps, her blue eyes shooting fire.

"I know." I smile at her.

"Then what are you smiling at?"

"You're always pretty, but fuck me you're gorgeous when you're pissed," I tell her before I pick her up from her seat and place her feet on the ground.

"Don't be cute when I want to be mad." She scowls at me, and it only makes my grin spread across my face.

"Let's go pack your shit."

"Yeah," she agrees, and I can see that she's not really mad. She wants to be with me; she said it last night, and I believe her. This is it. This is our shot. For real.

We head into her apartment that is appallingly bare. Other than sparse furniture and a few clothes, she keeps nothing here. In fact, I don't even understand why she lives here when I know she pulls a more-than-healthy income from the county as the medical examiner.

"When you grow up with nothing, you don't need anything," she whispers, and it hurts my heart so bad that I want to give her anything and everything she'll let me. I'm not rich, but I'm not poor either.

"You don't need anything," I reply. "But that doesn't mean I don't want to give you everything I can."

"Lee," she whispers, and her face is soft under the light of her living room.

"I know I don't have to," I say as I take her chin in my hand. "But I want to. So just let me have my way. Can you do that?"

"Yes," she says, and I feel like she's just given me the world.

"Then let me give you a home. A safe one with a big backyard, a kitchen where a family can come to-gether for dinner, and maybe in time, a surly cat that only likes you or a dog to run through that yard with our daughter."

"Yes."

"Then let's get your shit," I tell her before placing a hard kiss on her lips. "And after dinner, you can scour the internet for the perfect baby crib with rush delivery, because I think we're going to need some stuff and fast. Let's go home, make dinner, and then heat up my credit card a little bit on some baby stuff. Because even Claire has a crib, and I love her, but she's a fucking mess."

"You know all the baby planning in that house is Wes." She laughs. "Because Claire is a natural disaster. I bet if you looked right now, there would be Chinese cartons that molded over three weeks ago in her fridge."

"Truth."

"Let's go get my shit so we can go home," she agrees before taking my hand and leading me into the bedroom, where she packs a bag, and then we head home. It's too fast, I know, but it's also not. Emma and I have known each other for over a year, and it's all just finally clicking into place. Is it happening at warp speed? Yes. Am I going to stop it? Hell no.

I toss her bag in the back seat and lift her up into the passenger seat before climbing in and driving her home, holding her hand in mine the entire drive back across town.

I unlock the front door and lead her up the stairs and down the hall, into the master bedroom. I place her bag on the bed and pull her into my arms.

"Get comfortable," I say against her mouth before I deepen the kiss and show her that I mean it.

I stow my sidearm and badge in the safe in my nightstand before heading toward the dresser, where I keep my sweatpants. I strip out of my suit and dump it in the hamper before pulling my sweats up my legs. I don't bother with a T-shirt, because this is how I am at home. When I turn around, Emma hasn't moved from where I left her, and she has a dazed look on her face.

"What?" I ask.

"You're just really beautiful," she whispers.

"No," I say, shaking my head. "But you are."

"Stop it," she murmurs, and there is a delightful blush on her cheeks that is so innocent and beautiful.

"No," I respond as I make my way across the room and pull her into my arms. She curls into me, and I lean toward her, my mouth almost touching hers, when her stomach growls an unholy sound like a demented grizzly.

"Well, that's not at all embarrassing," she says.

"Don't be." I place a short kiss on her mouth. "I gotta feed my girl." Her stomach roars again, making me chuckle.

"Oh my God!"

"Just curious," I say, knowing it'll make her stop being so self-conscious. "Do you have a baby or a zombie in there?"

"A baby, you ass," she replies, slapping at my

shoulder but she does it with a smile on her face.

"Yeah, but I'm your ass." I kiss her again, because I just can't help myself.

"Yeah, you are." She grins. "Now feed me. The were-bear and I will be there in a minute."

"Were-bear?" I ask. "Is that a thing?"

"If you read romance novels, it is."

"Sweet. Whatever it is, I love it already," I tell her honestly as I leave the room, and I barely hear her reply.

"We love you already too."

I take the stairs two at a time and make my way into the kitchen. I pull a package of chicken breasts from the fridge and rinse them. I pat them dry with a paper towel before seasoning them. I drop some oil in a skillet and heat it up on the stove before dropping the chicken breasts in to cook.

I wash my hands with soap and water in the sink after wiping down the area where I prepped the meat. If there's one thing my mom taught me growing up, it's that a sanitary kitchen is a happy one and to clean as you go or be sorry after. Out of the two of us, I was the one who spent time in the kitchen with our mom. I'm not actually sure Claire can boil water without burning it. She's kind of like a natural disaster. I loved the time with my mom. I wonder if the babies—ours and Claire's—will grow up helping mom in the kitchen. There's nothing I want more than to make that a reality.

I grab a pair of tongs and flip the chicken in the pan before pulling some vegetables from the fridge. I wash and chop lettuce, onion, tomatoes, and a cucumber, tossing them in a bowl as I go. It's not a fancy dinner, but it's a healthy one. I make this meal often enough for myself to know it's satisfying after a long day.

I shut off the stove and pull the chicken out to rest on a wooden cutting board before I chop it, when I feel the change in the room. I know she's standing there, watching me. I would know Emma's presence anywhere.

She's wearing my T-shirt again but nothing else other than my thick socks as she leans against the doorjamb, and I have to swallow twice to clear my throat, because hands down she is the sexiest woman I have ever seen in my life just as she is right now.

"So," she says with a mischievous twinkle in her eye. "Is this how you stay in such good shape? Because I don't know if I can live a carb-free existence. We might have to break up."

"No." I smile at her as I open up the old-fashioned wooden bread box in the corner and pull out a bag of dinner rolls.

"You were just a little too prepared there, Cap," she says as I place two rolls on a plate before filling it with salad and topping it with chicken.

"I'm not taking any chances with you," I admit before pulling a tub of chemical-ridden margarine out of the fridge that I bought just for her, because she's not wrong; I do eat pretty healthy.

Emma just laughs at my admission.

I fill my own plate with salad and chicken but now carbs or chemicals and carry them both to the farmhouse kitchen table. I grab a couple bottles of water from the kitchen as Emma grabs napkins and silverware, and we both sit down. I tuck into my meal, but she just sits there for a second, looking at her plate with wide eyes, and I wonder what's wrong.

"This is… like, a lot of vegetables," she says, making me laugh. "What?"

"What are you, two?" I ask. "Try it."

"Okay," she says, poking at her salad with her fork before finally taking a bite. She chews and her face changes from hesitant to joy. "Holy shit, this is so good."

"Thanks." I smile at her and eat the rest of my dinner.

"I think I've been spending too much time with your sister." She laughs.

"Probably."

We spend the rest of dinner chatting about our day, but it's not awkward or weird; it's almost like we've been doing this for years. She helps me gather up the dishes and finish putting the leftovers in the fridge when we're done eating.

"Want to see your present now?" I ask her after I dry my hands on a dish towel.

"You didn't have to get me a present."

"I know, but you'll like this one," I say as I hold my hand out to her. She takes it immediately, and I lead her up the stairs and down the hallway, not quite to my bedroom.

There are four bedrooms upstairs, and only one of them is currently in use. I let go of her hand and push open the door. It's a smaller bedroom next to the master. The walls are plain white, and the floor is the same old oak as the rest of the house. It has a small closet behind a door, and a window that looks out over the side yard. And next to the window sits the only piece of furniture in the room, an oversized rocking armchair with a matching stool.

I look back at Emma while she stands in the doorway as a tear slips down her cheek. "Shit. Fuck, honey, I'm so sorry. I didn't mean to make you cry."

"I know," she cries harder, and I don't know what to do. Emma is not a crier. "I'm not crying because I'm sad. I'm crying because I'm so happy. This is the nicest thing anyone has ever done for me."

"Really?" I ask, wiping a tear away with the pad of my thumb.

"Really."

"You wanna try out your new rocker?" I nudge her gently.

"I really do."

"Okay," I say as I let her go so she can sit in her

new chair.

I watch as she slowly lowers her body and settles in, sighing as she does. The hem of her borrowed shirt rides up her thighs, and I can see the edge of her plain white panties peeking out from underneath. My cock fills, and I close my eyes and take a deep breath to try to stop it before it's staring her in the face. I want her to have this moment. A woman should get to make her nursery everything she wants it to be for her baby, and I want that for her.

"I'll paint the walls whatever color you want," I tell her. "I'll buy a rug or two for the floors, so they aren't cold on winter mornings, and I'll hang the curtains you want."

"What if I want pink curtains with roses on them?" she asks.

"I'll buy 'em, and I'll bust out a drill and hang the hardware," I answer. "I want my girls to have everything they want, everything they need in this house."

"You would do that for me?" she breathes.

"Honey, I would do anything for you and this baby, and any other baby we might have after."

"You really mean that," she whispers, the awe in her voice evident, so I give her the rest of the honesty that goes with it. Emma should have all of that and more.

"I really do."

"Okay."

"You want pink curtains with roses, baby?" I ask.

"I don't know."

"Well, you think on that while I run down the hall and grab my laptop so you can look at furniture and some other stuff we might need."

"Okay," she says softly. "But… can we go somewhere and look together?"

"Think you can scoot over and give me some real estate in that big chair?"

"Yeah," she says softly.

"Then I'll be right back."

I head down the hallway to the farthest room away from the master bedroom. It's the one I use as an office. It has a big wooden desk and a chair, bookshelves, and a sleek silver laptop that sits closed on the desk.

I scoop up the computer and head back down the hall with it under my arm. When Emma sees me, she scoots all the way over to the side of the big chair, and that will just not do, so I lower myself into the chair and scoop her up into my arms so she's sprawled half on and half off me.

"Comfortable?" I ask her as she lets out a huff and brushes her hair out of her face.

"Yeah."

"Good." I smile as I open the laptop on my legs and log in. I don't hide the keyboard or the password from her; I just turn it to her so she can open up some baby site with a funny name and start looking. I pull out my phone and open up the notes app. "So what do we need?"

"Umm…."

"You're a little lost too?"

"Yeah," she admits, rolling her bottom lip between her teeth.

"Well, then it's good we're in this together," I tell her.

"Yeah," she repeats, taking a deep breath before turning back to the computer.

"So let's start with the basics. Car seat?"

"I kind of like the sets that are a car seat, stroller, and car base," she says.

"Good start. Make sure it's a jogger," I suggest.

"I don't jog." She laughs.

"I know, honey, but I do." Emma gets this dreamy look in her eyes, and I know I must have done something right. Whatever it was, I want to do it over and over again, so she only looks happy like that for the rest of her life.

We pick a set and add it to our online cart.

"Crib or bassinet?" she asks.

"I think we need the room set up here," I tell her. "But I also think you might want a bassinet in the master bedroom while she's really little."

"I like that too," she agrees.

We add all the furniture to the cart, look at blankets, clothes, diapers, and we load it all. I pull my wallet out of the pocket of my sweatpants and pull out my credit card. I don't even give her a chance to pay for any of it. I know she can, and I know she works hard and has a great career that she kicks ass at, but this is me taking care of my family.

"We should have Wes and Claire over for pizza and a crib building party," I suggest.

"I'd really like that."

"Good, honey. We'll make that happen."

"This is really happening, isn't it?" she asks as I close my laptop and set it aside.

"Yeah, it is."

"We're really happening."

"We're happening," I tell her. "Now up and at 'em."

"What? Why?" She hurries to jump up.

"Because big things are happening for us, our lives are falling into place, finally, and I'm going to take you to bed now, but I'm not going to fuck you in our daughter's room, so get moving."

And she got moving.

Emma hopped up and let me take her hand and lead her into the master bedroom—*our* bedroom. She can decorate this room or any other in the house the way she wants. I just want her.

I take her in my arms and hold her face in my hands. I could look at her forever, but she's here in my arms now. If there's one thing life has taught me, it's that we don't know how long we have, so maybe we don't have forever, but we're here together now, and that's all I need.

Emma wraps her arms around my waist, and I lean down and press my mouth to hers. I want her, I need her, but tonight, I don't want a hard and fast fuck. Tonight, I want to worship her like she deserves. She sighs into my mouth, and I take the opening to deepen the kiss, licking into her mouth. She meets me at every level, her tongue tangling with mine and her fingers digging into my side.

I drag my shirt up over her body and toss it to the floor. I walk her back to the bed and help her sit on the edge. Emma and I were always combustible together, and she was always adventurous in the bedroom. Pregnancy could cause some limitations if we let it, but we won't. I want her more now than ever before, and I have always wanted her.

I drop to my knees in front of her and slide her plain white panties down her legs. I look up at her and let her see the hunger I know is burning in my eyes. She swallows nervously and then lets me part her legs gently with my hands.

I hold her like she's delicate and treat her like she's the only thing that's important as I taste her. I kiss her and lick her; I give her everything I have to give. And when her fingers tighten in my hair and I feel her come on my tongue, I stand and push my sweats down, letting them fall to the ground. I step out of them and grab a condom from my nightstand drawer, rolling it down my hard length.

She parts her creamy thighs for me, and I step between them, wrapping her long legs around my waist as I slowly slide in deep. I close my eyes and take a deep breath, and when I open them, I only see Emma.

I lean over her, bracing my weight on my hands on either side of her on the bed, needing to be as close to her as possible, even if her swollen belly prevents that right now. I grip the comforter tight in my fists as I slide out of her tight heat and drive back in again and again.

She makes the sexiest fucking sounds as she wiggles underneath me, meeting me thrust for thrust. I feel a tingle burn up my spine and balls draw tight as her pussy contracts around me, drawing me in deeper, and I let her orgasm pull me under with her.

I press a deep kiss to her lips and slide out of her heat. I miss the connection immediately. I scoot her up the bed and pull the covers around her.

"Can I have my shirt back?" she asks sweetly, and I look back over my shoulder to where she sits up in the middle of my bed with the covers pooled around her waist, her full breasts hanging heavy and unrestrained. She's like a wet dream come true, and she wants to cover it all up, so I don't even think when I answer her question.

"No."

And then I head to the bathroom to take care of this condom. When I'm done, I walk back into the bedroom and see she hasn't reclaimed my T-shirt, but she is under the covers now, so I peel them back and settle in before pulling her into my arms and holding her tight.

My last thought before sleep claims me is that this is paradise.

It's so fucking hot.

I hate this desert. I hate the sand that permeates everything. It's in my hair and my eyes and between my teeth. Sweat drips down my spine and from my forehead. I use the back of my gloved hand to wipe it out of my eyes, but the effort is wasted, because another just drips down right after.

When the tip came through the chatter wires that the terrorist we had been searching for was hiding in this village, a village we'd been near for months, I couldn't believe it. It seemed too good to be true.

I hold my rifle steady in my hands as I patrol. Posing as an infantry soldier to gain recon entry into the village was easy enough. We just needed to spot the guy and signal our sniper on the hill. Easy breezy, in and out.

But when we breach the walls of the village, one thing becomes clear.

We were wrong.

About everything.

There is no easy breezy, in and out. There is no one

living inside these walls. Every man, woman, and child has been slaughtered. Gunned down where they stood last.

A woman lays sprawled by a cart; her lifeless eyes are the only thing that peeks out from the scarves that cover her head. But it's the squirming coming from underneath her that has my attention. A kid, a young girl, pulls herself out from under her mother, a woman who must have sacrificed herself to protect her child. She's the only one living in this entire hell on earth that's left.

But when I look back at her mother, it's not her dark-brown eyes I see, but Emma's bright-blue ones that don't see me, no light left inside them.

"No!"

I try to get to her, but I can't. I'm frozen. It feels as if my legs are tied down and steel bands wrap around my chest and arms. And I can't catch my breath. I can't breathe.

"Emma!" I scream. I have to get to her. I can't lose her.

"I'm right here," she says, but I don't know how, because she's dead.

"Emma!" I cry out again. How could I have finally won her, only to have her taken from me like this? Is this my penance for the life I led before her?

"Lee!" Someone shakes me, and I blink my eyes

open. Fuck, it was dream. I had a nightmare with Emma in the bed with me. "I'm right here."

I sit up and gently dislodge her hands from my body. I bend my knees up around me and rest my forearms on them, dropping my head into my hands while I try to catch my breath. How could I have been so careless?

"Fuck," I bite out.

"Lee," she whispers, and I feel her gentle hand touch the small of my back.

"I'm sorry," I whisper. "I'm so fucking sorry."

"What do you have to be sorry for?" she asks as she settles into my side more firmly.

"I could have hurt you," I admit my worst fear.

"But you didn't."

"I could have though."

"But you didn't, and you won't," she assures, touching my jaw and forcing me to look at her beautiful face, and I can admit to myself that I needed to see with my own eyes that she's all right and not rotting in that village.

"You can't know that," I whisper.

"I do," she says with a strength in her voice that has my attention. "You would never hurt me."

"Not intentionally—" I start to say, but she doesn't let me finish. My woman is a warrior, and she won't let this go. I can see it in the way her eyes flare in the moonlight. It's sexy as hell.

"No," she says with confidence that I wish I felt, but my heart is still trying to beat its way out of my chest, and my blood is roaring in my ears. "You never would, and when you're ready to admit it, we both know I'm right."

"Emma—"

"How long have you been having nightmares?" she asks, changing the subject in a soft voice. I swore earlier that I would always give her the truth when I could, so I do exactly that.

"Always. Off and on, but not like I have been lately," I admit.

"Do you want to talk about it?"

"No," I answer immediately. "Not ever with you. I don't want to dirty you."

"Then with someone else?"

"I haven't before, but I will if you want me to," I tell her.

"Okay," she says softly. "Just think on it."

"Okay," I promise, turning to her and pulling her into my arms. I breathe in the strawberry scent of her hair and let it wash over me. I feel the tension in each muscle slide out, and I relax, if only a little bit. My pulse is still racing, and adrenaline is coursing through my body. I need to get up and run a few miles to keep the ghosts at bay. "You make me feel better. I'll just go run. You go back to sleep."

She looks at the bright blue glow of the digital

alarm clock on the nightstand. It's three in the morning. She could go back to sleep, but I'm up now for the rest of the day. I usually am after a nightmare like that one.

Emma turns back to me with her bottom lip firmly between her teeth. She lets it go before she gives me what's on her mind. "Maybe let me make you feel a little better?"

"Emma—" I start. I don't want her to feel like she's mine to use when I need to work something out of my system. She's more to me than just a body.

"I want to," she whispers as she scoots around me and settles between my thighs. Between the adrenaline mainlining my body and the attraction to Emma that won't ever go away, she has my dick's full attention when she reaches for it.

She wraps her slim hand around my cocks and pumps her fist around me twice, making me groan. And then she looks up at me, her blue eyes burning into my purple ones as she leans forward and licks the very tip of me.

The breath in my lungs burns, and I realize I've been holding it as I watch her pink lips, the same pretty pink as her nipples, slip around my cock, sliding up and down before swirling her tongue around my tip. Her hand fists my cock at the very base, and she slides it up and down in time with her mouth.

I'm lost watching her as she takes me deeper and deeper with each pass of her hot mouth, and my balls draw up and I rock my hips, but it's when I see her sneak her other hand between her legs to finger her clit that I realize she did want this. She wants me like I want her, and I'm only happy to oblige.

"Emma," I say her name, and my voice is sandpaper-rough as she swallows me down again. Her blues eyes burn me as I watch her get herself off while she sucks my cock. "Don't you dare come."

She gasps around my hard length, and I watch her move her fingers faster over her pussy. I growl, letting her know that is not how we're doing this. She wants to play, so we're going to play. She wants to come, then she can come on my cock, not her fingers.

I grab her by her arms and drag her up my body. She hovers on her knees over my cock. I steady her over me, and when I touch the tip to her opening, she sinks down on me. She's so hot and wet, fucking dripping, and there's nothing stopping her descent until her ass rests just over my balls, making us both groan.

"Did sucking my cock turn you on?" I growl as I skate my hands over her hips and up to her full breasts. I pluck her nipples hard between my fingers, making her gasp and squirm on my cock.

"Yes."

"Did you have fun playing?"

"Not as much as I would've if you'd have let me finish," she mumbles, but it turns into a moan when I roll my hips.

"Oh, you're going to finish," I tell her. "On my

cock with me deep inside you."

"Yes," she says as she rolls her hips, testing the movement. She lifts up, sliding off me before dropping back down.

"You want to ride my cock?" I ask as I flex my hips with her movements, driving deeper than before.

"Yes," she pants as she moves faster over me, and I place my hands over each of her breasts, letting my thumbs caress the hard peaks. She's so fucking sensitive there now, and I can't get enough of it. Emma puts her hands over mine, holding me there as she rides me, her movements becoming faster and faster. "I-I'm gonna—"

"Yes," I growl as I slip a hand out from under hers and grip her hip tight. Her movements become shaky as she nears her orgasm, so I thrust up into her as hard as I can, over and over, meeting each rock of her hips until she grips me so tight in her hot sheath as she comes I can't help but follow her over the edge into bliss.

I roll with her in my arms to the side as exhaustion weighs heavy on me, and I do something I have never done before after I've had a nightmare. I fall into a restful sleep and only wake with my alarm in the morning.

fourteen

two truths and an autopsy

I'm warm but not too hot. I'm safe and secure. And I feel... at peace.

For the first time in years, I did not wake up before my alarm went off. I hate to let go of the body I'm wrapped around, because she's warm and soft and exactly where I want to be right now.

"Make it stop," she groans in her sexy alto voice, and I reach over, and for the first time that I can remember, I hit the Snooze button and wrap myself back around her. "Mmm... that's nice."

I bury my face in the crook of her neck and take in the smell of sweat and strawberries on her skin. I press my lips to the back of her neck and pull her tighter into my arms. My cock thickens as she wiggles her ass back against it to get comfortable.

Everything with Emma is just right. We fit together like we were always meant to be like this. The only other part of my life that felt like it fit just right was my job, my duty to the department, the officers who work for me, and the people we protect. I always knew I was meant to be there. Just like I know I'm meant to be right here with her in my arms.

My alarm sounds again.

Sometimes duty sucks.

With a groan, I let go of Emma's warm, sexy body and silence my alarm for good this time. She takes the opportunity to burrow farther into the blankets as if she can hide from me, like I wouldn't notice her in my bed and not in the car on the way to the station.

"Not so fast," I say as I grab her ankle and pull her out of the bed with me.

"Nooo," she wails. "Just ten more minutes… or days… whatever. I'm not picky."

"You can sleep tonight," I tell her. "But you owe me one more body."

"I'll owe you a blowie if you let me go back to sleep," she says, and I'm not ashamed to admit that if my dick was in the driver seat, then that is definitely a deal he would make. He twitches on my thigh, and I let out a groan as the image of her on her knees with her pink lips wrapped around my cock fills my head.

"Change of plans," I tell her as I swat her naked behind, making her squeak. Her blue eyes open to glare at me. "You can suck me off, and then I'll fuck you in the shower before we go to work."

"Hmm," she non-answers as she heads for the shower. She might act mad at my dirty talk, but she's not. I saw the flare in her eyes before she turned away and headed for the bathroom.

I just watch her walk away with a smile on my face, knowing I'll join her there in a moment, but for now, I just need to say thanks to the universe for sending her to me. For the life we live and the future we have working together day in and day out, and then coming home to be together to raise this baby.

Life is perfect.

And then I walk into the bathroom to find her in the shower, steam clouding all around her. She stands under the hot spray with her head tipped back and her wet hair cascading down her back. She has her eyes closed and one hand braced on the wall, water rolling down her shoulders and over her full breasts. Her skin is flushed a delicious pink from the heat and from other things, and I watch with rapt attention as she slips her fingers between her legs.

"That is not the plan for this morning," I say as I grip my hard cock in my fist and step into the shower. I pump it in my hand as I watch her erotic movements.

"You took too long," she says just before her mouth parts on a gasp. Her climax is only moments away, and I step closer to her, letting her feel my cock in my hand against her side just before I lean forward and take her nipple into my mouth.

I cover her hand with mine and let my fingers sink

into her pussy. I pump them as she rubs her clit, and then her whole body tenses just before she detonates. I turn her around to face the shower wall and tip her hips back as I slam inside her.

Her fingers whiten where they press into the tile as I pound into her over and over again. Her walls continue to contract around me as her orgasm drives higher, and I couldn't stop if I wanted to.

She tosses her head back, her hair flipping over her shoulder and across my chest as she practically crushes me in her heat, and my name spills from her lips. I'm helpless to do anything but let her pull me over the edge with her, and when I do, it's everything; it's all-encompassing.

"We have got to have a serious talk about condoms," I tell her. "Or the lack thereof half the time."

She doesn't respond. She just stays slumped against the shower wall. I need to be more careful until we both have a clean bill of health. It's the responsible thing to do. Even if she can't get more pregnant, we should still be smart.

When our breathing slows but my cock is still inside her and my chest pressed against her back, she turns her head to the side, and without opening her eyes, she says, "I should have the autopsy results you want by ten."

I don't respond. I just smile. And then I finish washing us both before we get ready for work and I drive us both to the station.

And I do it all with a smile on my face, because life finally granted me everything I ever wanted.

I shuffle through the case files, adding notes, looking over Emma's findings and the crime scene photos, but I cannot find one link to each of the murders, including the Jane Doe. I rake my hands through my, hair, pulling at it. I know I'm missing something, but what?

At ten minutes to ten, I take the stairs down to the morgue. My heart beats a little faster knowing I'm going to see Emma, even if it's in an official capacity. I chuckle at myself. Who is this person I've become? I can't say it's a bad thing.

But it's not Emma who meets me in the hall. It's Wes.

"What are you doing here?" I ask my best friend.

"I just came to see if you need a real investigator on your baby-snatcher case," he says.

"You mean a fed taking over?"

"I mean me," he says with a broad smile.

"While I do enjoy your stellar company," I respond, "I can't help but wonder why."

"Because my badge is prettier?" he asks with a shrug.

"Doubtful."

"Because I'm more handsome?" he tries.

"Again, no."

"Because your sister is worried you're jumping life milestones like an Olympic equestrian?"

"Ding ding ding! We have a winner." I laugh.

"Fine," he says like it's no big deal. "I told her you'd be fine, but she worries."

"You mean she's bored and she likes to meddle?" I ask as I slap him on the back.

"Yeah, that exactly."

"Well, I'd love to have your input," I tell him honestly. "There's something about this case that I know I'm missing. I just don't know what yet."

"I'm happy to help," he replies.

"Great. I was just on my way to see Emma for some autopsy results," I tell him. A strange look passes over his face, but it's there one second and gone the next. "Well, shall we?"

"Uhh… yeah."

The door to the morgue is just a reach away, and I know that if I can hear an argument on the other side of the door, so can Wes. I reach for the doorknob, my reaction automatic reaction to jump in and rescue Emma, even if it's from my sister. But Wes lays a heavy hand on my shoulder to stop me. I look back at him, and he just silently shakes his head. It takes me back to all the times he gave me the same signal in the desert. I trusted him then, and I trust him now, so I wait.

"Don't you think it's time to tell him?" Claire asks,

her tone pleading, and I wonder what could have these two no-nonsense women so upset.

"I don't know how," Emma says. I can't stand the pain in her voice. My spine straightens when I hear it. She sounds so defeated, and I absolutely hate it. I hate that I think it might have something to do with me.

"Find the words," Claire warns. "This isn't like you, and it's not fair to him."

"What about Anna?" Emma barks, finally standing up for herself to Claire. But I hate the cause. Fuck, I hate what happened to Anna, but will she really be a wall between us for the rest of our lives?

"Do you honestly believe Anna would want you to behave this way and use her name to do it?" Claire fights back. "Lee's crimes were never egregious enough for this bullshit, and you know it."

"I'm scared," she replies, and I think now is when Claire will turn to her closest friend and offer her comfort, but she doesn't. Her reply is just as harsh as before.

"You should be, because when Lee finds out—"

But I don't let Claire finish that thought. It's time to put a stop to this, so I push the door open so Wes and I can walk in.

"When Lee finds out what?" I ask. The room feels wired. The tension coming off everyone is enough to light the room. Even Wes seems off put.

"Nothing," Emma rushes in to say, and I know it's

a lie. They weren't arguing about nothing, but I choose to let it go for now.

"Sure," I say with an easy smile. "What do you have for me on the autopsy?"

Emma visibly relaxes. She closes her eyes for a second and takes a deep breath. Claire looks pissed—granted, that's one of my sister's main emotions, so I don't put too much stock in it. I'm sure whatever it is they were fighting about is bad, but I'm not going to force the issue with Emma. We promised to be honest with each other as we move forward with our relationship. I have to walk a fine line and unite the family I was born to with the family I'm building with Emma, because I hope with everything I've got that we can just be one family at the end of the day.

Emma picks up a file off her desk and flips through it quickly before handing it off to me. I open it up so I can follow along as she explains her findings to me.

"Beth Anderson, thirty years old, was found in her home," Emma begins, and it's like she's a completely different person. Gone is the woman who was scared and unsure, and in her place is an intelligent woman who has earned her place in her field and has the confidence to know it. I breathe a sigh of relief to see her more herself than before. "She was injected with atropine, as were the other two victims."

"Cause of death?" Wes asks.

"Exsanguination," Emma says bluntly. "She bled out once her baby was removed and the incision site was never closed."

Wes's face pales as I know mine did when I first made the connection between the victims and the women who stand in the room with us now. It's not a fun connection to make.

"Sounds like we have a bad guy to catch," Wes says quietly.

"Absolutely."

"And the babies?" he asks.

I answer with the only word I can. "Gone."

"No trace?" he asks.

"Not a one," I reply. "We cannot find any link. Each victim was essentially abandoned by their families, so no one is looking other than us. The babies are gone."

"Fuck," he bites out.

"Yeah."

"Maybe we should take this to your office," Claire suggests after a moment, and I can't help but wonder why we need to go to my office. She leans in and whispers to Emma, "He should be in his territory."

What the fuck is going on here?

"Is that what you want?" I ask Emma.

"Yeah," she says sadly, not looking at me, and I hate it.

"Then let's go," I tell her gently.

Instead of taking the stairs, we ride the elevator up to the bullpen and walk through the room. It almost feels like a death march. Even Wes knows something terrible is coming, and I am the only one who doesn't. I open the door, and everyone walks into my office. I close the door behind us and stride around to my chair, needing to put some distance between me and my family.

I sit down and take a deep breath before saying, "The truth. Now. What's going on?"

"Now, before things get crazy," Claire says, holding up her hands in front of her, "just know that pregnancy hormones make you do really stupid shit."

"What did you do?" I ask quietly.

"Well…" she hedges.

"It's not her. It's me," Emma admits, her blue eyes pleading for me to understand, but what, I don't know. "I was afraid to tell you about the baby."

"It's not like I didn't know. I can see you're pregnant with my own eyes," I explain, hoping she will put me out of my misery and tell me what's going on here.

"I know," she says softly. "You know what you wanted to talk about this morning? In the shower?"

I look to Wes and then Claire before responding. "Do you want to talk about this now?"

"Yes, Lee," she says. "You're safe, because there hasn't been anyone else."

"I know not now, but before." I look at her. I don't understand.

"No, Lee," she murmurs. "Not ever. There was no

one after you, and no one before you."

"I don't understand."

"The baby is yours," she says softly.

"We talked about this." I smile. "I already told you that I'd raise the baby as mine. She's mine with or without my blood."

"I know. But it doesn't matter."

"So she's mine," I say. Not a question but a statement. One that is starting to become clearer, and I'm not liking what I'm hearing.

"Yes, but it also already was, because I haven't slept with anyone but you," Emma states clearly for everyone in the room to hear.

I lean forward and brace my hands on my desk for support.

"What about that guy?" I ask. I saw them together, both here in the station and in restaurants. I felt like I saw them together everywhere, and it was driving me fucking insane. I was so jealous, so devastated that she would choose that guy over me. Not that I think I'm the be all, end all, but I love her. I fucking love her, and she lied to me. The thought hangs heavy between us.

"He wanted there to be something between us," she says, looking me in the eyes so I can see the truth of her words, even though it feels too little too late. "But I couldn't. He wanted me to give up the baby so we could be together, but I didn't want that. You know, because you saw him here, giving me a hard time about it. He wanted it, he wanted me… but I also couldn't go there, because he wasn't you."

"So you were just going to keep my daughter from me?" I ask quietly, too quietly, and Wes knows exactly what that means, as his frame stiffens and he goes on alert. No one says a goddamn word. "Answer me!"

"Yes," she whispers. "I was going to keep her from you."

"Why?"

"It doesn't matter why," she cries. "I was wrong. I know that now."

"It does matter!" I shout. "Why did you hate me so much that you would keep my only child from me?"

And she whispers the one word I should have known would be the truth behind all this mess. The one name I knew would keep coming up between us time and time again, and I just didn't want to admit it.

"Anna."

"You were never going to give me a chance, were you?" I ask. "You were never going to give us a chance?"

"I was wrong," she says.

"Oh, I know you were wrong," I say cruelly, wanting to inflict as much damage as she has done to me, whether it's right or it's wrong. Right now, I'm laid bare and bleeding all over my desk for everyone to see. I don't care who hurts right now, because I'm hurting, and I don't think it will ever stop. "But that's not what

I asked you. I asked if you were ever going to give me a chance."

"No."

Before the word is ever out of her mouth, my coffee mug, half filled with liquid that's long since gone cold, is in my hand and then hurtling across the room, where it smashes against the side wall. Emma flinches but stands there, waiting for me to inflict more damage.

"I was wrong, Lee," Emma pleads. "I'm so sorry. You have to believe me. I'm so sorry."

"I don't know what to believe," I respond. It's not the right thing to say, and we both know it, but she's kept me from everything. From every doctor's appointment and every ultrasound. I was a silent observer for months while she lived her lie.

"Please." Tears flow unchecked down her face as she begs me to understand, but I just don't know what to do. I feel cold; I feel numb. I wonder where we go from here and if I can ever trust her again.

And then my world stops on a goddamn dime.

Emma gasps and clutches her belly before dropping to her knees. I stand up, sending my chair hurtling back into the wall behind it, and I'm leaping over my desk as Wes and Claire rush to her, but we're all not close enough. In her panic, Emma moved into the room between them and me, so we all watch in horror, me with a front row seat, as her beautiful blue eyes, ones I thought I would get to look into every day for the rest of my life, roll up into the back of her head and she drops unconscious to the ground.

Wes pulls his phone out of his pocket and dials, but I'm not paying attention. I scoop her up in my arms and think that maybe she's right after all; maybe I do deserve to be punished, because every woman who's ever loved me dies, and it looks like Emma is next on the list.

"I need a bus to Precinct 528!" he shouts. "We have an unconscious pregnant woman, age thirty. She showed signs of distress before collapse."

"I'm so sorry," I whisper as I hold the only woman I've ever loved in my arms. "This is all my fault. I'm so fucking sorry."

"The ambulance is on its way," Wes says, but I know it's too late. Emma does not regain consciousness the entire time we wait.

It's too fucking late.

And it's all my fault.

fifteen

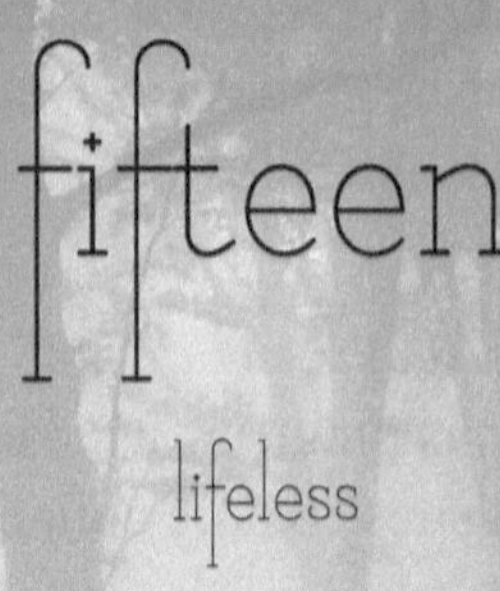

lifeless

"**S**ir, you need to step back."

Wes grabs me and hauls me back. I don't know how I move, how my body functions; I just go where he leads me. But the entire time, my eyes stay glued to Emma's limp body.

She's not dead.

Those words Wes spoke just before he took her from my arms rattle around in my brain, echoing over and over again. But she still isn't here either.

I don't even know what happened. One minute, I was yelling, trying to come to grips with my life and how the one person I love above all else could hate me so much that she would make moves to keep my child from me. Even knowing I missed out on having my big sister in my life before she was murdered, because her mother had done the exact same fucking thing to my dad. But then the next minute, she was on the floor.

She looks so still, so lifeless.

She's not dead.

I held her in my arms until Wes shouted, "Back here!" when the paramedics came in and took her from me.

Wes and I watch as they load her onto a gurney and run her through the station, where every officer in the department stands silently watching, to the waiting ambulance. It's a hero walk if ever there was one.

I climb into the ambulance behind her. It's like I have no control of my body. I have to be with her.

"I'll meet you at the hospital," Wes says just before they slam the ambulance doors behind us.

I sit with my head hanging and tears streaming down my face, holding her hand. The ride is silent. I don't speak. I'm not sure I can, even if I tried, and Emma never wakes.

The paramedics talk quietly back and forth, and their radios squawk from time to time, but I don't listen. I can't listen. In my head, I'm screaming, and that drowns out all the noise.

The emergency room staff is waiting for us at the ambulance bay. I jump off quickly when the door opens and get out of the way as they unload her gurney.

"What do we have?" a doctor asks.

"Female, age thirty, pregnant," the paramedic rattles off, and I want to shout that her name is Emma Parker, she's a fucking brilliant medical examiner, that baby is mine, and I'm hopelessly in love with her. Please save them both. But I don't. I stay quiet, gritting my teeth. "Showed signs of distress before she collapsed at work."

"And you are?" she asks me. I have to clear my throat before I answer.

"Captain Liam Goodnite," I inform them. "I'm her partner."

"I wasn't aware the patient is a police officer."

"She's not," I answer. "She's our medical examiner. What I meant was she's mine."

"Oh. Right this way," a nurse says, taking my arm.

"No," I say, digging in my heels to stop as I watch them wheel her down the hallway. "I want to go with her."

"I know," the nurse says gently. "But you can't go with her now. Someone will come get you when we know more."

And then she shoves me in a small waiting room of crying people, and I lose all hope. How could everything have gone to shit so fast?

For the first fifteen minutes, I pace. It's like my feet can't be still. I can't make them be still. There's an endless amount of energy pooling in my body. It's dark and ugly, and there's no other way to get it out of my body than to move. It's like with a snakebite; you have to suck out the poison. Only this poison is endless in its supply as it slowly withers something vital inside me until it curls up and dies.

I stop in front of a window; it looks out over the parking lot, but I don't see the cars or the asphalt. I don't see any of that. What I do see is the way her blue eyes sparkle when she smiles at me. I see her blonde-and-pink hair spilled over my pillow the very first night I had her and knew then that I never wanted anyone else. I see the way she threw her head back as she came for me under the dock on the beach. I see her joy over that damn nursing chair in a room just for our child, in a house that was mine but is now ours. And I see the pain etched across her beautiful face as she begged me to forgive her just before she crumpled to the ground.

And there was nothing to forgive. I was angry and hurt that she would keep something that big from me, but in the end, she's only human, I'm only human. But I could still see with my own two eyes that she was fragile, that she was breaking apart, and I pushed her anyway. And then she broke for good.

"Are you all right?" I ask Emma as I jog the last few steps to catch up with her as she's making her way across the parking lot of the California Diner. We're here to meet Claire and Wes, who swear they have some big news to share.

"Yeah," she says, looking a little sad. "Why wouldn't I be?"

"I don't know, honey. You tell me."

"There's nothing to tell, Lee," she murmurs, and

the way she says it has me thinking there is really a lot to tell. But I'll let her have this play. She'll tell me when she's ready, and I'll be here waiting for her. I'm not going anywhere.

I hold her hand in mine as we make our way to the big-glass front door of the diner that has looked like a giant silver twinkie for as long as I can remember. She pulls her hand from mine just before I reach for the door, and I barely hold in a frustrated sigh. Since the night I made her mine under the dock after my sister's wedding, we have been together. Only, she doesn't want anyone to know. At first, she said we just needed to give it some time, but now I'm afraid she's never going to be ready, and I'm not feeling all that fucking great about being someone's dirty little secret.

"Your party is right this way," the hostess says before leading us to a table where Claire and Wes are already seated. I chuckle when I get a good look at my sister, who has had questionable taste in food since she was a kid and spent the last thirty years building her love affair with junk food. Now, she looks like she's just been rescued from a deserted island and will eat the fucking menu if she doesn't get food soon.

"Hey!" she says, jumping up to hug both Emma and me.

"So, how was the honeymoon?" I ask.

"Italy was amazing," Wes says with a smug smirk on his face.

"Oh gross," I tell them, making a gagging noise.

"That's my sister, asshole."

"No, that is my very sexy wife." Wes chuckles.

"Okay, that was kind of gross, Wes," Claire says.

"Too far?" he asks playfully.

"Just a smidge," she replies, holding up her thumb and index fingers about an inch apart.

"My apologies," he says on a not at all feeling guilty smile. The fucker. He's lucky he's my best friend or I'd punch him in the face. Again.

The waitress comes and takes our order, and I settle on the double cheeseburger and extra fries. Emma asks for chicken noodle soup, but she just pushes it around in her bowl. Come to think of it, she's not looking that great. I hope she's all right.

"Are you feeling all right?" Claire asks her softly, but I hear the concern in my sister's voice, and it only serves to make me worry more.

"Are you sick?" I ask Emma.

"I'm fine," she answers, but the look on her face says she's anything but. "So what did you call us down here to tell us?"

Claire leans back in her seat and looks at Wes before answering. "I'm pregnant."

"No shit." I laugh. "I thought you were just fat."

"You asshole," she grumbles while Wes laughs. "Why do I like you again?"

"Because I'm your favorite big brother."

"You are my only big brother," she corrects me with a smile on her face. *I love my kid sister more than just about anything, and the feeling is clearly mutual. Even with the gap in our ages, we grew up close.*

"And I'm really happy for you, kiddo," I tell her with emotion ringing in my voice. *"But for real, you are looking kind of fat."*

"Nice knowing you," Wes mumbles.

"I'm not fat, you nutsack! I'm having twins!" she shouts, making me laugh.

Emma looks around a little uncomfortable before seizing her opportunity to escape. "I guess I'm not feeling well after all. I should go," she says before tossing a twenty on the table and practically running for the door.

"What was that all about?" Claire asks me. *I just let out a frustrated sigh.*

"I just don't know. We were fine until about a week ago, and then she just stopped calling and started looking really sad again. I can't get her to talk to me," I admit. *I don't know where we went wrong. I thought we were building something, but clearly, I was wrong like always.*

"Well, I'm sure you'll figure it out."

"I will," I tell her, *but in truth, I'm not so sure. What I do know is that Claire doesn't need to be stressing about me. "Don't worry about me. I'm happy for you guys."*

"Thanks, Lee," Wes says, shaking my hand as I stand and drop a twenty on the table. And then I walk out of the diner.

I should have known. Something was obviously up with Emma months ago. I should have been paying more attention, not lost in my own self-pity. She asked for time to come to grips with being an us, and then… there was no us at all, and I had just let her drift away.

But I will not make that mistake again.

I grip the window ledge tight in my hands and drop my head forward. I can't stop the images of her in the ambulance, all pale and lifeless, to when they took her from me here. They play on a loop through my head, and I hope to God it isn't the last time I ever see her face.

And then I do something I haven't done in a long time. I pray.

I don't know how long I stand there, lost in the wind, until a heavy hand on my shoulder pulls me from my thoughts. I look to see who it is, and I'm not surprised it's Wes. We've been friends for a long time. The sad look on his face takes me back to the day my five-year-old baby sister Claire wandered out of the woods behind our house. She had been missing for days, and the police had started to give up hope, and then there she was, running like her life depended on it—and now we know that it did. She was so tired and malnourished and filthy that she stumbled and then collapsed right into my best friend's arms.

I will never forget his voice ringing out, *"Lee! I got her!"*

I look past Lee and see my sister, now his wife, wringing her hands with tears in her eyes.

"She'll be okay," she says quietly to me. I can't trust my voice right now, so I just nod my head once.

Behind her stands my parents, my niece Brooklyn, and my little nephew Seth. Their older brother Eric is deployed with the Army. Claire and I didn't know we had a sister named Bonnie until she was murdered over a year ago, but her children are with our family now. I wish with all my heart that we could have known her, and it will always cut deep that we didn't, but I am so thankful we know the kids.

I feel a warmth flow through my chest at the sight of my family. It's like a huge weight has been lifted off my shoulders.

"What are you guys doing here?" I ask.

"Wes called," my dad answers, and I look to my brother-in-law.

"We're family." He shrugs. "It's what we do."

"Thanks, brother," I tell him, and I have to clear the emotion from my throat.

"Let's sit," my mom orders out of the chaos of our entire family in this waiting room.

She hustles us all to the group of open seats at the back of the room. One look around shows me the room is full of pockets of families huddled together while they wait for news. I was alone before, but now I'm not. Emma didn't have anyone, but now she has all of us. If she pulls through, she'll be a Goodnite for the rest of her days.

"Come sit by me, Liam," my mom says as she pats the chair next to her, and I lower myself into it. I feel decades older than my forty years. A heavy sigh falls from my lips.

Claire lowers her belly-heavy body into the chair on my other side. Wes stands back and leans against the wall, watching as she grabs my hand in hers and squeezes it tightly. Her entire life, I've looked after Claire. Being eight years older than her, it was always my job to protect her, to comfort her when she needed it, and now here she is, comforting me.

"She's going to be all right," Claire leans in and whispers to me. I squeeze her hand twice quickly, our secret code for *I love you*.

"You're a great kid sister."

"I know." She smiles at me.

"Papa," Seth says to my dad. "Can I have a snack?"

"Sure, buddy," Dad answers. "I think I saw a vending machine on the way in, and I know I could use a cup of coffee. Anyone else?"

I shake my head, and everyone else answers for themselves. Brooklyn jumps up to go with Dad and Seth. At nineteen, she's studying her undergrad classes at a local community college, but she just told my parents that she's transferring to a school in San Diego in the fall. Like the rest of us, they're sad to see her go but so ready to watch her fly.

I watch as the doors swing closed after Dad leads the kids through to the snack machines. Silence settles in around us, and I want that; I need it. I need to be alone with my thoughts. I need to be ready so I can face whatever is happening with Emma. I need to be ready to be there for her and the baby, whether she wants me there or not, because they need me, and I need them.

I let my head hang forward, and I close my eyes, focusing on the pattern of my breaths in and out of my lungs. And all the while, I hang onto my sister's hand like a lifeline. She's the only thing keeping me grounded while my world is spinning out of control.

And then I hear the doors swing open.

I think Dad is back with the kids, so I don't open my eyes. That is, until the shouting begins.

"I need to see someone right now!" Jerrod, Emma's douchey ex, shouts, and I open my eyes. What the fucking is he doing here?

"What the actual fuck?" Wes clips out, mirroring my own thoughts.

"Sir, can I help you?" a nurse asks, and I can see by her body's posture and her alert eyes that she is uncomfortable with his outburst. I am too, and a quick look at Wes and Claire show the same.

Fuck.

"Yes," he answers crisply. "I am the significant other of a woman in your care, and I need an update on her immediately."

"He can't mean…." Claire whispers.

"And who would that be?"

"Emma Parker."

"He does," Wes practically growls as the nurse looks to where my family and I sit.

"Ms. Parker's family is here already," she informs him hesitantly, and I stand in case I need to be ready.

Jerrod looks at me, and his eyes flare. He clearly didn't know I would be here. "That man has nothing to do with her. I am her boyfriend, and I have to tell you that time is of the essence."

"And why would that be?" the nurse asks just as an older woman who looks familiar approaches them.

"I need you to save the baby," he bites out. "Now. Emma is gone, but my child is not."

The breath seizes in my lungs.

"I assure you," the nurse says, "now is not the time to make those decisions."

"I have already made them," he snarls.

"No fucking way," I growl. Wes grabs me from behind as I try to move forward. "You want to just let her die?"

"She's already gone," Jerrod says.

"No, she's not!" I yell. "You don't fucking know

that."

"It's my right to make these decisions on her behalf," he says, turning to the nurse. "I have documentation."

"I'll need to see that," the nurse says.

"Here," he replies, handing her the paper. "It's a copy."

She looks up at me, and there's a sad look in her eyes. Shit. Fuck, fuck, no. She thinks it's legitimate, and he's going to let Emma die and take the baby? That doesn't make sense after I heard him push her more than once to give the baby up.

And then it dawns on me where I know the older woman from—the adoption agency.

"Why do you want the baby delivered so quickly?" I ask.

"Madame Driskill is here to take custody of the child," he says.

"You're giving the baby up?" I ask quietly, too quietly, and Wes knows it, because his hands tighten on my shoulders.

"Of course," he answers. "It's the right thing to do."

"No, it's fucking not," I practically shout.

"You don't have a say here," he snaps, and I hate his haughty fucking tone, but I'm about to shut him up, because there is no way I would believe this asshole over Emma.

"Oh, but I do." I give him a lethal sneer, and I hear Wes chuckle.

"I don't see how," Jerrod replies.

"The baby is mine, not yours," I tell him.

"You're lying."

"I'm not, and we both know it," I tell him, Wes, the nurse, and anyone who is listening. "Emma swore to me only this afternoon that she had never slept with you. Ever."

"They will never believe you," he snarls.

"It's a quick DNA test," the nurse adds, and I smile at her. She did not like the idea of not trying to save Emma.

"We don't have time," Madame Driskill snaps.

"It'll take a lot longer if I have to bring you in for kidnapping the child of a police captain," Wes drawls. "The FBI frowns on that kind of thing."

"Well, I never," she pouts.

"I'll get a cheek swab," the nurse says.

"I'd appreciate that," I tell her gently before she hustles out the door.

Wes and I stand facing Jerrod and Madame Driskill, when the doors whoosh open one more time. I don't look up, because I'm sure it's the nurse coming to swab my cheek for DNA that they will match against Emma's baby from a sample through her womb. It's a simple enough procedure, and if it keeps this asshole away from my woman and my baby, the sooner the fucking better, but it still seems shitty that this asshole is here forcing an unnecessary procedure because he wants Emma's baby all of a sudden. I just don't understand why he's that bog of an asshole.

But it's not the nurse, and I know by the deep voice that calls my name.

"Captain Goodnite?"

"That's me," I say, turning to the doctor in scrubs, looking exhausted. He holds my whole world in the palm of his hands, and I won't know if he's about to break my heart with his words or not.

"Emma Parker is asking for you."

"She's all right?" I ask, and my voice is rough. I have to clear my throat a few times to get the words out.

"She is," he answers. "She's a little out of it and needs her rest, but you can go back and see her for a bit."

"And the baby?"

"Still cooking like she should be." He smiles at me for the first time, and I feel my breath whoosh out of my lungs.

"Thank God."

"I'll take you to see her now," he tells me, and Wes pats me on the back.

"Thank you." I follow him to the door, and when he moves to unlock it with his badge, I look back over my shoulder and see Jerrod and Madame Driskill are gone.

sixteen

you scared me

"**S**he's in here," the doctor says as he pushes on the big silver handle of a hospital room.

"Thank you," I say, but once I look through the door, I lose my voice.

Emma is lying in a hospital bed. Her blonde-and-pink hair is dark and matted with sweat around her forehead, and it's a stark comparison to her pale complexion. She's paler than usual, and I hate it. She looks so small, lying there in the middle of the bed, and I can't help but feel like this is all my fault. I'm the one who put her here.

And then slowly, her baby-blue eyes flutter and then finally drift open.

"Hey," she says softly, and her voice is scratchy.

"Hey, baby," I say softly, and I can hear the emotion welling up behind my words.

"I'm so sorry," she whispers, and it's then that I move to her. I can't be standing across the room from her when she's laying it all bare like this. I grab a chair from over by the wall and drag it to the side of her bed.

"No, baby," I tell her, my voice strong and sure, and I take her cool hand in mine. "It's me who's so fucking sorry."

"Lee—" she starts, gripping my hand in hers.

"No, honey, I fucked up."

"But so did I," she says.

"Yeah."

"Can we…?" she trails off, and I wonder if she's fading in and out like the doctor said she would. But when I look up at her beautiful face, it's scrunched up, and her eyes are on me.

"Can we what?" I ask as I use the pad of my thumb to smooth out the wrinkle she's making between her light brows.

She takes a deep breath and then answers me. "Can we move on from this?"

"I hope so," I tell her honestly. "I love you, Emma."

"I love you too," she says, and a tear runs down her cheek. I swipe it up with my fingertip.

"No tears, baby." I take a deep breath and lean farther into her, gently touching my lips to hers. "I don't know what the future holds for us, and I have no crystal ball. But I know that what I feel for you, how much I love you, I have never felt for another."

"Lee—"

"I love our baby, and I have never met her," I continue. "And I know that if we work at it, we can have a beautiful life. But I also know that will not happen if we do not trust each other and give each other honesty at all times. Can you give me that?"

"Yes," she whispers.

"Because I can give you that easily," I tell her honestly. "I would give you anything in my power."

"Lee, honey," she whimpers, lifting her hand to touch my face.

"I just need you to love me."

"I totally do."

"That's good, baby," I tell her. "Because you scared the shit out of me today."

"I scared the shit out of me too," she says. "If I'd lost the baby—"

I cover her rosy mouth with mine for a quick kiss that was more about stopping the flow of words from her mouth than passion. "You didn't."

"But what if—" she tries again, and I cut her off.

"No," I say firmly before laying my hand gently on the swell of her belly. "You didn't. She's all right. Safe right her in your belly. We can't think past that."

"But—"

"No," I state firmly. "That path leads to nothing but darkness. Stay with me here in the light."

"Okay," she whispers.

"Now tell me. Are you here with me in the light?"

"Yes, Lee," she answers. I can tell by the look on her face that she sees how serious I am about this and lets it go.

"Good, baby," I say before I drop another kiss on her lips. "Now let's talk about scaring me like that."

"Lee," she hisses as she eyes me. "I didn't do it on purpose."

"Oh, I know," I tell her and let the wicked smile spread across my face. "But still. I think we can come up with something."

"Now, let's not get ahead of ourselves."

"I think a lot of rest and books and some movies are a fitting punishment," I tell her. "I hear absolutely terrible things about that tiger documentary, so it's probably right up your alley."

"Come here, honey," she urges softly.

"And baths and foot rubs…"

"Please, baby," she begs. "I need you to come here and hold me."

Emma scoots over on her bed to make room for me, and I carefully climb in and pull her into my arms, while being mindful of the tubes and wires coming off her. "Anything for you, Emma. Anything in my power."

"I know," she says quietly. "But I just need you."

"And our baby."

"And our baby," she agrees.

"We really need to give her a name," I reply with a smile on my face so she knows I'm not mad.

"We really do," Emma agrees, and then she drifts off to sleep in my arms before I have a chance to ask her about her ex's power of attorney. But I don't even care, because right now, everything is right in my world.

seventeen

nightmares and new normal

*E*yes.

The smell of sulfur fills my nostrils, and smoke sears my lungs. The heavy weight of the rifle in my hands is like second nature to me. I could carry it in my sleep. During training, I probably did.

But it's the eyes that chill me to the bone in the middle of this hot desert.

I don't know how the intel had gone so bad. I know it happens, but not like this. One minute, the mission was going to plan, and the next, the world exploded. Spurts of gunfire can be heard all around me, but it's the screams that ring in my ears.

"Fuck, fuck, fuck!" I hear Adams scream through the comms in my ear. "They're dead. They're all dead."

And he's right. They're all dead. Every last one of them. I was helpless to prevent this, yet still I feel like I should have. It's as bad as if their blood was directly on my hands.

I make my way through the village we've been watching, my heart in my throat. Buildings, homes, the carts in the market, they're all gone, burned out shells of what they were before. And bodies crumpled where they fell. Men, women, children—death does not discriminate. Their eyes vacant after life left them.

If eyes are the windows to the soul, then this is a portal to hell as I look at the faces of each person who should not have died. A child we gave a candy bar to yesterday, an old lady who offered coffee in the market, and a beautiful young woman whose belly was swollen with a baby.

Her dark eyes watch me, haunt me, as she sees me and nothing at all. And then they change to the brown of Ashley Horner's, her belly cut open and her child just gone. I was helpless to stop her death too. I didn't know her, and she still died.

The smoke burns my throat as I turn to the left and see Emma's blonde-and-pink hair, her blue eyes open and watching me, her beautiful body mutilated because I was in her life.

"No!" I shout.

But the eyes of the dead scream that this is all my fault.

"Lee!" someone shouts. I don't know who it could be. It sounds like my girl, but I know it's not, because she's dead and it's all my fault. It's all my fucking fault.

I should have trusted my gut not to trust the intel. Jake said time and time again that it didn't feel right. Something was off. Rick, Wes, and I all agreed. It was off. But still. I should have known. It's my fucking job to know this village was harboring a terrorist, that they weren't safe, even the women and children.

I should have protected them. It was my job to protect them.

And now they're all dead.

"Lee, baby, come back to me," someone says as my body is forcefully shaken, and a small hand grips my shoulder hard.

My eyes blink open, and I stare into the concerned blue eyes of Emma. Not dead. She's not dead. She's alive and well…. Well, seeing as she's currently in a hospital bed, that is a relative assessment.

Fuck.

I had another nightmare, and they're getting worse.

I blink again and sit up. It takes me a second to get my bearings and realize where I am. I'm in a hospital room, but it's not my room; it's Emma's.

And then it all comes rushing back to me.

We were in my office at the station, and she was talking to me. Wes and Claire were there as a buffer, because they had known what was about to go down. They knew. Emma knew. I did not know, and what I did not know was that she lied to me about the baby she carried. When I found out she was pregnant a few weeks after she had broken it off with me—again—only this time without a reason, I had asked her point blank if the baby she carried was mine, and she lied to my face. And then she compounded that lie by lying to my face about it every day for the last seven months. And like a fucking idiot, I believed every word out of her mouth.

Even after I busted my ass to make her mine again, this time for keeps, she still lied. Until yesterday, when she came clean and I lost my mind, because it fucking burns to know she would do that, knowing how I felt about her all along.

And then she collapsed, and my whole world ended. Because even if it burned like nothing else, even if she cut me like no one ever had, she was still mine, and that baby in her belly is still mine. I'm still in love with her, because she is it for me, and it was my job to protect them. But I did not do that, and it fucking burns to know that. In a way, I know it will always burn deep in me.

"Hey," she whispers.

"Hey," I whisper back.

"You came back to me," she says in a way that I know she means more than just I left the dream world for her, but that some seriously heavy shit went down between us and I am still here with her. So I answer her the only way I can—truthfully.

"Always."

She closes her eyes, taking them away from me as

she angles her face to her lap, but not before I see the tears welling in them.

"Baby," I murmur. I keep my voice soft and gentle. It's a shit thing we have to get through, but I don't ever want to hurt her again. Never again.

"I'm so sorry." She sniffles.

"Baby, eyes." I need to see her eyes, and I need her to see mine, to see this is real and it's happening, but we have to put this hurt behind us first.

"I'm so fucking sorry," she cries.

"Emma, honey," I say a little firmer. "Give me your eyes."

She looks at me instantly. And when she does, I see the tears she's shed for me dripping down her pink cheeks, and that is one more cut that scores across my heart where Emma Parker is concerned.

"Baby, don't cry for me," I say softly as I press my palms to the sides of her gorgeous face and use my thumbs to wipe away her tears, but they're falling faster than I can sweep them off.

"I can't help it," she says as more fall.

"I guess I'm just going to have to find a way to stop the tears and make you smile," I tell her just before I press my lips to hers. I kiss her tears away, and it is deep and wet and hungry.

Someone clears their throat behind me, and I pull back, but I don't let her go. Her face is bright red in her embarrassment at getting caught making out like a couple of teenagers, but it just makes me grin at her. She's mine, and I don't give one fuck who knows it. Emma takes one look at my shit-eating grin and rolls her eyes at me before I look over my shoulder to see her doctor stepping into the room.

"While I do advise you keep my patient happy—" He smirks. "—I don't think you should make her too happy for about three to four days… if you catch my drift."

"No orgasms," I reply. "Got it, Doc. Anything else?"

"Kill me now," Emma mutters under her breath, but it's loud enough for me to hear it, and I throw my head back and laugh. I do it knowing that for the first time in a long time, my soul feels lighter.

"I wouldn't say no orgasms," he says. "Sexual activity should be all right as long as it's not too… rigorous."

"Sounds good, Doc." I wiggle my eyebrows at her.

"Kill. Me."

"No can do, gorgeous," I say, winking at her. Emma just sighs.

"Here are your follow-up instructions," the doctor says, handing me a neatly stapled stack of papers. "If you have any questions, feel free to call me, and definitely follow up with your OBGYN, but otherwise, I see no reason why you can't go home."

Home.

I didn't get it before, but now, I do. Home is wherever Emma is. I'll follow her anywhere, and I will die before I let her be hurt again.

"The nurse should be in shortly," he says. He turns back just before he leaves the room to look at us, where I'm holding Emma's hand tight in mine. And he says something so softly I almost don't hear him, but I do, and I know Emma does to by the hitch in her breath. "Take care of each other."

"Will do, Doc."

I carefully peel back the covers and help Emma dress in the pair of my sweatpants and my favorite AC/DC tee that's a million years old. I know for a fact Emma has been trying to steal it for a while now, and I keep taking it off her body and putting it back in the drawer. Of course, whenever I would have to divest her of my favorite tee, I would soften the blow by making love to her.

Now, all evidence suggests she shared her plight to steal my shirt with my sister, who aided and abetted her in her endeavors by packing it in a bag for Emma to wear home and by bringing no other options, including Emma's own actual clothing.

I can't help the smile that spreads across my face when I realize what Claire has done for my girl. Fuck me if it doesn't make the scars seared into my chest feel a little lighter, knowing my family still has her back, because that means they also have mine.

And then the nurse comes in with a wheelchair,

and I lift my girl in my arms like a bride and place her in the seat. When the nurse tries to take control of the chair, a rumble bubbles up from my chest, and she wisely steps back.

I loaded her up in my truck and then drive her home.

Home.

The place where I can take care of her. A place to be a safe haven, a shelter in the storm, one where we can raise our children and I can keep them secure.

Only I would find out later—much, much later—and much too late that it wasn't.

eighteen

hungry

Three days later

"Are you hungry, baby?" I ask, and I have to bite the inside of my cheek to keep from chuckling at the obvious side-eye I'm getting from my girl.

"Yes," she says, stretching out the "s" to hiss like a snake. It's not the only sign of her displeasure since I brought her home from the hospital.

It all started when I decided to follow the doctor's instructions to the letter. Emma thought as long as she kept a low profile, she could go back to her lab. Not. Fucking. Happening. No, my woman was going to stay home with her feet up and rest. This caused an argument. Well, a one-sided argument, because I decided I was never going to raise my voice in the same room as Emma ever again. Maybe even the same building. I could probably drive to New York if I had to yell. At the time, these all seemed like rational conclusions.

I had visions of Emma lounging around and reading our baby classic literature in the womb. I would wait on her hand and foot, and she would be well-rested and healthy in no time. Emma had other plans. She saw this as not a vacation but a prison. She did not want to rest and be waited on; my girl was in a mood to build her nest before her chick hatched.

Every day, it was something new. I would find her standing over the bed looking down at the instructions to fold some super stretchy sheet into a baby carrier. The next day, I about lost my mind when I found her washing every baby outfit, blanket, and tiny little sock.

We had another row over that one. I wanted to do everything and wanted her to do nothing taxing. Apparently, that was boring. She lamented her plight to my sister, who came over one afternoon so I could go into the station, because the secrets of the baby-snatcher case were still eluding me, the entirety of my department, and the FBI.

Claire had brought over a—*gasp*—Hawaiian pizza, because pregnant women apparently think pineapple on pizza is appropriate, and some romance novel with a bare-chested highlander on the cover that our mother had given her when she was recovering from being shot. I grumbled the appropriate amount about my woman needing a bare-chested highlander, when Wes laughed and informed me that sexy books turned women on and that book is "inspiring," his word, not mine. After my lunch stopped trying to retreat on me at the thought of my sister being inspired in any way, I went home to find out for myself.

And that is how I find her now, lounging on the sofa with the book open and cover rolled back. Emma is lost in the book and turning the pages pretty damn fast. But the part that has me most fascinated is the way she absentmindedly rubs her legs together from time to time like a cricket.

My girl finds her bare-chested highlander book *inspiring*.

Thank fuck.

It's been several days since she was released from the hospital, and she's been hinting for the last forty-eight hours that she's ready to end this self-imposed dry spell. She moved from hinting and vague innuendo to downright demanding dirty, dirty things from me. And it's all I could do to hold back. I needed her more than ever after our fight in my office, but I'm not about to put her health or that of our daughter at risk.

The doctor said three days, and today is the fourth since she was released.

Dry spell over.

She's so engrossed in her book that she doesn't notice me come in or lean over the arm of the sofa, so my mouth is close to her ear when I ask, "Are you hungry, baby?"

"Yes."

I can barely contain my smile. She's irritated with

me for not giving in... on anything. On her wanting to do heavy lifting or going back to work. I would not eat pineapple on my pizza, and I wouldn't give her my dick until she was well enough, and that pissed her off.

And it was sexy as hell.

"What do you want to eat?" I ask her, knowing the answer, because there's only one food group she'll entertain in her current state.

"Pizza."

"I knew you'd say that," I tell her before pressing my lips to the corner of her mouth. I let the tip of my tongue touch her skin for just a second, making her gasp before I pull back like I was never there. "What kind do you feel like tonight, baby?"

"Barbecue chicken," she replies, and I wonder not for the first time if she was abducted by space aliens in the last six months. We do not put barbecue sauce or fruit on pizza. Ever.

I do not say this though. Instead, I press another kiss to her hair and mutter, "Anything for you, honey." And then I pull my phone out of my pocket and order the love of my life another crime against pizza.

After I place our order, I leave her to her book in the living room. I jog up the stairs and lock up my sidearm and badge in the safe in my nightstand drawer. I shuck my clothes in the hamper, or really, the area around the hamper. I need to do laundry and bad. And then I pull on a pair of sweatpants, the gray ones Emma hasn't confiscated yet, and I think she only lets me have them because she likes the way my dick looks in them. But to be fair, I like the hungry way she looks at me in these pants.

I take the stairs two at a time as I pull my T-shirt down over my head. I hit the bottom of the stairs just in time to hear the doorbell sound. I pay the kid delivering what may prove to be the worst pizza known to man and carry the boxes back into the house.

"What do you want to drink, honey? I ask after I pop into the living room and drop the boxes on the coffee table.

"I can get it," she answers quickly as she snaps her dirty book closed. I take a closer look at her and notice her cheeks are flushed and her full breasts rise and fall with every flustered breath she takes.

"I got it," I say softly. I hide my reaction to her arousal. "What do you want?"

"Umm... ice water?" she asks, fanning herself. "Is it hot in here?"

"I don't think so. Maybe you're getting sick."

"No, no," she says. "I'm fine."

"Okay," I reply, hiding the smirk that plays on my mouth at the sight of my poor girl trying to hide her reaction to a book.

I make my way into the kitchen and grab two bottles of water and a couple plates and napkins. When I get back to the living room, Emma has moved to sit up on the sofa. Her legs are crossed underneath her as she sits in the middle, waiting for me, and not for the first time, the sight of her takes my breath away. She's in a pair of my sweats and another shirt of mine. Her blonde-and-pink hair is knotted up on top of her head, and my fingers itch to pull it down and mess it up. Her face is washed clean of makeup.

I sit down next to her and hand her a plate and a napkin. Flipping open her pizza box, I grab three slices and drop them on her plate before taking her water bottle and twisting the cap to open it before closing it again so she won't have to struggle with it.

"Thanks, baby," she mumbles as I set her water down on the coffee table within her reach.

I just nod before filling my own plate. I reach for the remote and turn on the television. The voice of the local news anchor fills the room as the screen fills with a picture of me before panning to a clip of Wes walking out of the local FBI office.

"Local authorities still have no leads on the baby-snatcher case," she says.

"That's right, Martha," the male co-anchor says. "The killer is still at large."

I flip the channel again, and the sounds of a stadium fill the room as a ball game shows on the screen. I lower the volume and watch as a kid from Texas comes up to bat. I let myself get a little lost in the sound of the crack of the bat and the cheers and let the stress of my case leave my body.

"Whoooa, Doctor!" the announcer calls. "That is

out of here!"

At some point in time, Emma and I set our plates aside, and she settles into my side as we watch Dallas beat New York. It's not too late when the game ends, and I shut off the TV. Emma is so relaxed and curled against me that I wonder if she's asleep.

"You awake, honey?"

"Yeah, Lee," she says as she sits up and brushes the hair that's fallen out of her top knot back from her face with a practiced hand.

"Let's get ready for bed."

"Okay," she replies, looking at me, and I almost drown in the way her blue eyes heat at the thought of going to bed.

"Let me just pick up real fast," I tell her as I gather the empty pizza boxes and water bottles destined for the trash. She stacks our plates and carries them into the kitchen to rinse in the sink while I take out the garbage.

The downstairs is picked up, the lights are out, and the house is locked up in a matter of minutes, and Emma and I climb the stairs hand in hand. When we make it to our room, I turn on the bedside lamps while she takes her turn in the bathroom to brush her teeth and wash her face. I follow her in after and brush mine. I love the domesticity of getting ready for bed with her. She's comfortable here in my home—*our home*—and I love everything about her settling in with me

I follow her out of the bathroom and turn off the

light before stripping off my T-shirt, I toss them toward the hamper. I think maybe our relaxing evening on the sofa put her in the mood to curl up and sleep, maybe cuddle a bit.

And it's not until I see her climb up onto the bed on her hands and knees that I realize I assumed wrong.

Somewhere from the bathroom to now, Emma kicked off her stolen sweatpants and panties. As she climbs onto the tall bed, my shirt rises over her full hip, and I can see the glistening pink of her pussy. It's enough to make my mouth water, but it's the sexy siren look she tosses over her shoulder at me as she takes in my reaction to her arousal that pulls a growl from me.

"Did you have your fill of your barbecue, baby?" I rumble as I watch her body move.

"Yes, Lee," she whispers. "Why?"

"Because now I'm hungry, and it's your turn to feed me." I hear the hitch in her breath at my words, and I drop to my knees next to the bed. I grip her hips in my hands and pull her ass back to hang over the edge as I part her seam with my thumbs and fuck her with my tongue.

"Yes, Lee," she hisses as I lick and kiss and suck every inch of her that I can get to. I missed the sweet taste of her and the way she gets off for me in my mouth.

She grinds her pussy against my mouth, and it's not long before she has the sheets twisted in her fingers and her head thrown back as she comes.

I gently help her lower down so that her breasts rest against the top of the bed and she has to turn her head to the side. With her lush ass in the air and her pussy dripping for me, I push my sweats down my legs and step out of them.

I rub her back gently and love the noises that fall from her lips. I let my hands slip down every few passes to brush against her inner thigh or occasionally her pussy, making her whimper and moan as she arches her back and reaches for me.

And then I slide a finger into her. She gasps and rocks against my hand, and I pump my finger a few times before sliding it out.

"Lee," Emma starts to grumble, but she doesn't have time to release the words I know are on the tip of her tongue because I plunge deep inside her before she can utter a single word. "Yes!"

I pull back, letting my cock slip almost all the way out before thrusting back in again and again. I grip her ass cheeks in each hand and push them apart so I can watch her take my cock, and it is the sexiest fucking thing I have ever seen.

"Lee," she pants.

"I love watching you take my cock."

"Yes." Her voice is high-pitched and breathy as she reaches closer and closer to her climax.

"Show me how much you love taking my cock," I growl as I pump in and out of her, and she digs her hands into the mattress and pushes back, making me drive harder and faster until she lets go with a keening cry.

I grip her ass tight in my hands and drive deep before I follow her over the edge.

I slowly glide in and out of her, rubbing the small of her back as we come back down to Earth, and I slip out of her and drop my lips to the back of her neck as I tip her to her side. I make my way into the bathroom and grab a washcloth. I take care of my girl before I lift her into the bed to lie back on the pillows.

I toss the washcloth into the bathroom before climbing into our bed and curling Emma deep into my side. When she settles into me, I say, "I don't think that was the mellow, less energetic session the doctor had in mind."

And then I get to fall asleep with the musical sound of Emma's laughter still ringing in my ears.

Everything was perfect and it was exactly the way it was supposed to be. It was like the stars aligned and the universe finally said, *"This is exactly where you're supposed to be. You made it through hell, and here is your reward."*

But little did we know everything was about to change.

nineteen

everything i ever wanted

My dad always says, *"The days are long, but the years are short."* He means when Claire and I were growing up and how fast it all really happens, but when you're in the thick of family life, it doesn't feel like that. It drags on.

But I don't feel that way.

I feel like there will never be enough time with Emma and our children. I feel like I can never make enough memories. And I feel like I don't know where the hours in the day went when I lay my head on my pillow at night.

But I also know this is everything I've ever wanted.

Having grown up in a happy home with two parents who not only loved each other but doted on their children, that was the only type of family I ever dreamed of. But as I got deeper with the SEAL community and then with the police department when I came home, the darkness consumed me.

After a while, I didn't think I would ever find my white picket fence and the woman I was meant to grow old with. And that coupled with the fact that I spent twenty-five years watching my baby sister turn into her own darkness, I began to wonder if our parents weren't the gold standard but a rare occurrence.

And then my childhood best friend decided Claire was the one. Their path to each other was rocky, to say the least, but now they have it all. Watching it unfold and seeing them get to a solid place made me realize I wanted that too. I found the one I wanted to grow old with, but while I was drowning in my own darkness, I missed it. I fucked up the order, and it had cost me everything.

But not anymore. Emma is back in my bed and in my life, and we are building a beautiful future. Will it always be easy, smooth sailing? Absolutely not, but I wouldn't want it that way either. It's not real life, and what Emma and I have is as real as it gets.

And with that thought, I turn to her sleeping body and settle in to show her just how real we can be.

"Did this shit come with any instructions?" Wes growls.

"Uh oh," Claire mumbles. "Maybe we should go order more pizza. Or buy more beer."

"Bourbon, babe," Wes rumbles. "This shit calls for

bourbon."

"Wes—" she starts, and I watch as Emma bites her bottom lip. I look to my feet so I won't laugh at her reaction to Wes, but I can't stop the smile that plays out on my face, because one, she's cute as hell, and two, he's not wrong. It would appear the beautiful, painted light-gray nursery furniture we picked out is not that easy to put together.

"I would even take instructions in Spanish, German maybe," he continues to grumble. "But this is like a goddamn mime wrote it. And in fucking hieroglyphics!"

"Wes," my sister warns.

"There are no words!" he shouts. "It's just pictures that a monkey fucking drew!"

That's when I lose it. I throw my head back and roar with laughter, because he's funny as hell, and then I pull my girl into my arms and drop a kiss to her lips to soften the blow of my best friend being pissed as hell at our choice in baby furniture.

"Don't worry," I whisper. "He's all bark and no bite."

"I heard that!" Wes snaps, making Claire laugh.

"I'm not sure we're talking about the same man," Emma mumbles back.

"We'll get it built," I promise. "Why don't you and Claire go catch up."

"Okay."

"And order some pizzas?" I ask as I hand her my wallet.

"Okay."

"And try ordering some without fruit or any other weird shit."

"I will not promise that," Emma snaps. "But I will try."

"That's all I can ask."

Once the women left the room, I took up the instructions for the tall dresser and sent Wes to look over the crib, which proved to be much easier than the dresser—the instructions written in mime hieroglyphics.

And a few hours later, the room is filled with a heavy wooden crib, a tall dresser, and a short one with a soft pink diaper changing station on top of it. The pink floral sheet Emma picked out and I ordered is on the mattress, and a small stuffed elephant and blanket are nestled in the corner, waiting for my baby girl. Wes is hanging pictures, large pink flowers, and a giant ruler on the wall so we can measure her height as she grows. I'm hanging the long pink curtains with huge, sweeping ruffles that made my girl smile when she saw them.

"Well, I think that's it," Wes says as he steps back to take in the room.

"I think so too," I agree.

"Never thought you'd be the kind of guy to have a girlie-pink baby room in your house, brother."

"Me neither," I agree, with what has to be a dopey smile on my face. "But I didn't know it was everything I ever wanted."

"Yeah." He smiles. "I know the feeling."

"I know you do," I remark.

"And enough of the girl feelings bullshit," he says, clapping his hands. "Before I start my period."

"Thanks, asshole." I laugh.

"Anytime, brother," he says, slapping me on the back. "That's what I'm here for. Time to show your lady."

"Yeah."

"Emma, Claire!" he shouts. "Show time!"

"Classy as always," I say, rolling my eyes.

"What?" he prompts with a chuckle. "It works."

"What is it?" Claire asks, sounding a little worried, but it's Emma's reaction I'm looking for, and she does not disappoint.

Her beautiful face softens, and she whispers, "Oh my God." I know it's everything she's ever wanted, and my chest burns with pride, because I am the man who gets to be the one to provide that for her. I am one lucky bastard and I know it.

"Come here," I tell her, my voice gruff with emotion, and again, she does not disappoint when she walks straight into my arms and I hold her tight to me.

"We'll just be uhh…" Claire trails off.

"We're going to put these tools away and give you guys a moment," Wes fills in.

"Yeah, that," Claire agrees, and I don't even nod to acknowledge them. I only have eyes for Emma.

"Do you like it, honey?" I ask her quietly.

"Is the Pope Catholic?"

"Are you happy?"

"This is the happiest I have ever been in my entire life," Emma admits, and I can't help but place a soft kiss on her lips.

"Grateful I'm the man who gave that to you," I tell her.

"You've given me everything, Lee," she says as tears fill her eyes.

"No tears," I order gently. "You're the one who's given me everything I ever wanted."

"I'm glad, baby," she whispers before clearing her throat. "Now, we better go find your sister before she has too much time to snoop around the house."

"That's unfortunately true," I agree.

And Emma and I walk hand in hand through the hall and down the stairs, but Claire isn't snooping, something we both know she loves to do. Claire and Wes are standing in the living room with a giant pink bow on a well-worn and slightly battered bassinet.

"Is that—?" I ask.

"The Goodnite bassinet our Grandpa Goodnite

made before you were born?" Claire asks.

"Yeah, that."

"Then yes, it is," she says with a smile.

"You don't want it?" I question. "I figured you'd use it."

"Wes and I agree you guys need a little family love to start you off right," she says gently before changing her tone, because my sister is not comfortable with outward displays of emotion. "Besides, all the baby books say twins need to be in the same crib, and this isn't big enough."

"Of course," I murmur before pulling my sister into my arms. "You're the best sister I could ever ask for."

"Well, obviously," she says, but even though she tries to hide it, I can hear the sniffle as she cries. One look at her overprotective husband, and I can see he hears it too, so I pass her off to his care and he wraps her up in his arms. "God, these hormones are a real bitch."

"Sure, baby," he says to her. "You show them what a real badass you are."

"Sleep with one eye open, O'Connell," she snaps, pulling away from him.

"You know I'd rather sleep dick-deep in you, baby," he growls.

"All right, well this has been real fun, and I appreciate your help, brother," I say, clapping my hands. "But there is no sexy talk about my sister in my house, so get the fuck out."

Emma just laughs before hugging Claire. "Thank you," she whispers to my sister.

"Of course," Claire says with a wink, and then the door closes behind them and they're gone.

"Happy?" I ask, pulling my girl back into my arms.

"Yes."

"How happy?" I ask, letting her see the heat in my eyes.

"Very," she answers.

"Then why don't you take me upstairs and show me just how happy you are? I suggest.

She clears her throat before answering. "I suppose I could do that."

"You suppose?"

"Why don't you follow me and find out?"

And then she takes my hand in hers and leads me upstairs to do just that.

twenty

Three days later

"**B**abe, just go."

I let out a frustrated breath. I need out of this house, and I know without a doubt that I am driving Emma apeshit hovering over her, but I am so damn scared that something will happen again. I can't lose them after I've only just gotten them. But clearly, my worrying is not doing Emma any favors, and I get the feeling she's politely trying to tell me that if I don't get out of this house and out of her face, she's going to punch me in mine.

"I'll be all right," she promises, and I know I should ease up, because she is the one who suffered; she is the one who ended up in the hospital, not me. But at the same time, I'm the one who held her limp body in my arms and thought, *Not again.*

"I know," I say and shove my hand through my

hair. In my head, I know that she's right; she's going to be fine if I leave her for a few hours to go see my sister, who is also on the verge of committing marital homicide against her overprotective husband. "I know."

"It's just lunch," she says, laughing. "Besides. It sounds like poor Wes needs a break more than you do."

I smile, because she's not wrong. To say that my buddy/brother-in-law is nervous about becoming a dad would be a massive understatement. Add to that his wife is carrying twins in a high-risk pregnancy, and he's a fucking basket case, and after she almost died at the hands of a madman last year, I can't say I blame him. So when Claire sent up smoke signals and carrier pigeons that she wanted sprung from her mansion prison for some emergency mu shu chicken, Emma and Wes jumped on the idea. Wes, because he knows I would die myself before letting anything else happen to Claire and their babies, and Emma, because she wants me out of this goddamn house so she can get a moment alone.

So Wes is swapping working the baby-snatcher case for me in exchange for me taking Claire out to lunch. This mission plan is twofold. One, it keeps her out of trouble. Claire is a brilliant detective, but she's a fucking mess with too much time on her idle hands. And two, because I'm fucking stuck. I know there's something, some key detail I'm missing in this case. I've been searching through all the files, I've re-interviewed every witness, including those pertaining to the Jane Doe who kicked off this whole mess, because I know in my gut they are all related, and nothing.

Not one damn thing.

So really, this break is for me too, because if this case doesn't crack soon, I might. And with everything going down with Emma and me, that cannot happen. So to keep it together for my family, for my job, I agree to leave this house when it's the last fucking thing I want to do on a Saturday.

I push out a frustrated breath before turning back to my girl and pull her into my arms. Her belly is so big now that she can't press into me like she likes to do, but at the same time, I can feel our daughter in between us, and I fucking love that. I love her. I love them both. So I'll do what she needs and get out of her hair. I can let go for a little bit, I mean, what's the worst that could happen?

"Okay," I say as I press my lips to the top of her head.

"Okay?" she repeats hesitantly.

"I'll get out of your hair for the afternoon." I look to her face and see she's smiling. "I'll only be gone for a few hours. That's not enough time to get to Mexico."

"It is a decent head start though," she says with a smirk.

"Not funny," I warn, but it's an empty threat and we both know it.

"Maybe I just want to see what the punishment might be before I commit the crime."

"If you want me to stay home and play, baby, then just say the word," I tell her and watch her eyes dilate. My girl likes to play, but at the same time, she really does need an afternoon to relax, and I can see the two warring emotions play out across her face. "Maybe a raincheck tonight?"

"Yes," she whispers just before I press my mouth to hers for a quick kiss.

I let her go so I can run back upstairs and tuck my feet into a pair of running shoes and grab my wallet and cell phone out the little bowl on my nightstand. I slip my drop gun into the holster at my ankle and head out of our bedroom.

Emma is puttering around the kitchen when I make it back downstairs. She's making herself a cup of tea while classical music is playing in the background. The whole scenario is like one from an alternate universe, because I never in my wildest dreams thought I would ever see badass Emma Parker making tea and listening to sonatas.

Although, there is a frown playing on her gorgeous face.

I come up behind her and wrap my arms around her before touching my lips to the corner of her mouth. She settles into me immediately, and I love that.

"Why the long face?"

She lets out a frustrated sigh. "The baby prefers Mozart to Def Leppard," she pouts, making a smile spread across my face.

"Well, we have the rest of our lives to impart your spectacular musical taste on her and all the babies who come after," I tell her, turning her around so I can kiss her deep and wet.

"All the babies who come after?" she asks, and the surprised look on her face is so fucking adorable.

"Sure."

"How many babies are we talking about here?"

"As many as you want," I answer.

"As easy as that?" she asks. "Just whatever I want?"

"Yep." I smile. "It's as easy as that. I just want to build a family with you, and we're already doing that, so I'm set."

She looks at me for a long time, studying me before blurting out, "I want four. Two girls and two boys, but I would take any combination."

"With you, that sounds like a beautiful family," I say softly. "I can't fucking wait."

"Well," she says after a beat. Emma pats me on the chest quickly and blinks back the wetness in her eyes. "You better get going so you can come back and hover some more."

"Har de har har," I say, rolling my eyes. "Maybe when I get back, I'll let you hover for a change, over my dick."

The pupils in her blue eyes flare again, and I feel my dick thicken as I watch her lick her lips. Fuck me, my girl wants to ride my dick.

"You better go," she whispers.

"Yeah," I say. "I have my phone on me if you need anything."

"I'll be all right." She smiles. "See you later."

Emma follows me to the front door, and once I'm through it and heading to my car, I hear it close softly behind me. And then I drive to pick up my sister and take her to lunch, knowing the whole time I'm gone, she'll be there when I get home, and nothing could be better.

"I'd like two orders of mu shu chicken, a cup of hot and sour soup, and an order of the cream cheese wontons," my sister says delicately to the petite waitress at Imperial Dragon who cannot imagine one woman eating that much.

"I'll have the same," I say, handing the server our menus.

"Are you really going to take all that down?" I ask, because it really is a lot of food, even for Claire, who has always had an appetite that most women don't.

"Of course I am," she replies, affronted. "It's like my own brother doesn't even know me anymore."

"You have to admit it is a lot of food." I laugh.

"It is," she replies seriously. "But I am eating for three."

"Is that even a thing?"

"It is!" she snaps before settling back in her side of the padded booth. "Besides, what about you, Mr. My Body is a Temple?"

"What about me?" I ask with a laugh.

"That's a lot of food?" she mimics.

"All right, all right," I tell her. "Now tell me what kind of havoc and mischief you've been stirring up since I booted your ass from my station."

"You didn't boot my ass from the station," Claire says incredulously. "I was put on a light bedrest! There's a difference, you know."

"Oh my mistake." I smile.

The waitress loads our table down with food, and Claire and I both tuck in. The soup is hot and tangy and just what I wanted. And truth be told, I was really over pizza and all of Emma's pizza disasters. I'm not entirely sure I could watch her eat pineapple on pizza again. Last night, it was pineapple, bacon, and anchovies. That's just not right, so today's lunch is just what I needed.

I watch Claire laugh at some story she's telling about how she drove her husband to the brink of insanity—again—and doing it smiling. I'm happy to see her so blissful in her life after all she went through when she was a kid and the darkness we didn't know she kept locked inside all this time. Now that Wes is in her life, it's like the light she had as a kid is back, and I will always thank him for bringing her back to us, even if I don't understand how or when she grew up.

"What are you thinking about with that look on your face?" she asks me.

"I was just wondering when the cute little kid I taught to hit baseballs and patched skinned knees on grew up," I answer. "I swear you were just baby in a little pink blanket Dad placed in my arms and told me it was my job to protect you for the rest of my life because you were precious."

"Lee—" My badass sister sniffles.

"Obviously, he didn't know what a hellion you'd turn out to be," I finish, since we're both uncomfortable with too much shared emotion.

"Asshole!" She laughs.

"Seriously," I say. "You're all grown up, and I don't know where the time went."

"Well," she says primly. "You and Wes were avoiding me."

"Yeah." I smile at her happily, and she just rolls her eyes at me.

We finish our meal with lighter conversation about babies and how our mother and grandmother are living their best lives planning for the impending arrival of more Goodnite kids. We talk about our late sister Bonnie's kids and how great they are, how we think Brooklyn is a way better student than Claire and I were, seeing as she was just accepted to a big university in San Diego. How she had just told our parents and our mother will cried, and our dad also cried but he also tried to hide it even though we all know that he's a big softy and that family is everything to him. We talk about how Eric is doing well in the army, and how scared that makes us at the same time we're both so fucking proud. And how the baby, Seth, is the spitting image of me as a kid and is also funny as all hell.

I pay the bill when it comes, because Claire told me it was my duty as her big brother to pick up the tab, which I was going to pay anyway, but still. I laugh when she promptly points out she didn't even bring a wallet with her.

And then we visit for another moment or so until a pained look slashes across her face.

"Claire?" I ask, because I know in my heart something is wrong with my kid sister, and I'm not sure what I can do.

"Lee," she whispers as she grips the edge of the table in her hands, her knuckles turning white as her body begins to quake. "S-s-something's wrong."

I push out of my seat and come around to her side of the table when she lets out a cry that rips my heart in two. What the hell is happening?

"Let's get you to the hospital, honey," I say calmly. That was one of the things I remember from our early emergency training: Always keep calm and speak in a soft voice. "Can you stand?"

She tries to push up but falls forward, gripping her belly instead.

"I need an ambulance!" I shout as I pull my sister into her arms.

"I'm on the phone with 9-1-1 now!" someone yells.

"It'll be okay," I tell her as I hold her in my arms like I did when she was a baby and brush back her dark hair that matches mine and our dad's before his turned gray.

"Okay," she says quietly as tears track down her face.

"I promise."

"It has to be okay, Lee," she cries. "Wes won't survive it."

"It'll be okay," I repeat. What I do not say is that she is absolutely correct. If something happens to Claire or their babies, Wes won't survive it. He was in a bad enough spot after she was kidnapped from their wedding rehearsal. He and I raced like madmen through the dark to get to her when we realized what happened. He wouldn't be able to take anything else.

Fortunately, we don't have to think on things for too long, because then the paramedics show and load up my sister.

"It's too soon," she whispers, clutching my hand in the ambulance after they load her up. I climbed in right behind her. I wasn't about to send my sister on her merry way to the emergency room. When they realize who she is, because GWT is a small town, they get us to the hospital faster than I thought possible.

Claire is taken into surgery the second we hit the hospital doors. The doctor took one look at her and whisked her away.

I call my parents and Wes, and then I wait.

I'm always fucking waiting.

Wes was in the field working the baby-snatcher case, so by the time someone got to him, he was rolling in here on two wheels and a panicked look on his face that we all shared. A nurse handed him a paper jumpsuit and made him promise to keep his underpants on, and then he was rushed away.

"How long do these things take?" my dad asks the nurse.

"Oh… about thirty minutes to an hour," she says with a smile. Unfortunately, that's the last smile we see from the hospital staff for a while, because Claire takes a turn for the worse in surgery.

The babies aren't that much better.

Wes comes out a short while later, still in his paper suit but now covered in what has to be my sister's blood, and his face is pale and scared. He looks up at me, and I stand instantly, making my way to him without thought.

We walk down the hall toward the nursery window and see them pull the blinds quickly as doctors and nurses work on two tiny babies to keep them breathing.

"What happened?" I ask as he leans his weight on the now covered window.

"I don't know," he says, closing his eyes. "One minute, she was fine, and the next, it was like the light in her was just gone."

"Is she…?" I can't bear to ask.

"No," he whispers. "At least not yet. They made me leave the room. Wouldn't let me be with her. My wife could be dying ,and I'm not fucking there!" he growls, his voice hoarse, and tears track down his angular face.

"And the babies?"

"Not breathing."

Two words. Two fucking words no one wants to hear. I don't know what to say to the man who was my oldest friend until the day he married my sister and became a brother, so we just stand there in silence together.

"I can't lose them," he says. His voice no more than a pained whisper.

"You won't."

"I don't know how I could walk in here a husband of one and a father of two, and now I could be leaving with fucking nothing," he says. "Without them, there's nothing left of me."

"It's going to be okay," I tell him the same words I gave Claire earlier, and I hope to God it's not a lie. As soon as we have word on Claire, I'll call Emma, but if my sister isn't going to make it, I'm not going to tell her best friend over the phone, I'll go home and tell her face to face so that we can deal together. But that's not going to happen. I refuse to believe that it's even a possibility.

"Yeah," he says, but I can tell by his tone he doesn't believe it either.

We stand there for another hour before a nurse comes into the hall and says, "Mr. O'Connell? We've been looking for you."

"Yeah?"

"You can see your wife now," she says with a smile that Wes is too far gone to see it does not say *"sorry your wife just died."*

"Is she?"

"She gave us a scare, but she's doing all right now.

"And the babies?" he asks, and I hold my breath again.

"Still looking pretty rough, but I think they'll be all right too," she answers.

"Thank you," he says to me while following the nurse.

"Any time."

"Go get your girl," he calls back before the metal doors close behind him, and I don't delay in doing just that.

As soon as I step back into the hall to say good-night to my family and tell them all is well, my phone dings with a voicemail. I must not have had service deep in the hospital. I pull it out of my pocket and see I missed a call from Emma. She probably wants to know what kind of disgusting pizza I want for dinner tonight.

But when I put the phone to my ear to listen to her voice message, everything changes, and not for the good.

twenty-one

got it from your mama

"**H**ey, honey, it's me. I know you're out with your sister, but I haven't heard from you in a while. I hope everything is okay. *Anyway, that's not why I'm calling. I just got off the phone with the state lab, and they said the hair you found at the crime scene is a mitochondrial match to the defensive wound DNA found under Jane Doe's fingernails. Anyways, let me know if you'll be home for dinner. I'm feeling like pizza. Shocking, right?"* And then she laughs her throaty chuckle that warms my heart and makes my dick hard. *"I love you, Lee."*

I hear the click as she disconnected with my voicemail and then nothing. I'm tired. It's not only been a long fucking day, but it's been a long fucking two weeks, so my brain is playing catchup. It's like I'm wading through quicksand or deep underwater.

And then something she said clicks in my brain.

"The hair you found at the crime scene is a mitochondrial match to the defensive wound DNA found under Jane Doe's fingernails."

The hair at the crime scene... The hair at the crime scene...

Oh my fucking God, the hair I pulled off her douchey ex-boyfriend when we had words at the station. I told Emma it was found at a crime scene when I passed it off to her to run it. And now it's a mitochondrial match.

But that's not a *match* match, so what does that mean?

I press the Call Back button from my voicemail app and put my phone to my ear. It rings and rings, and then I hear, "You've reached Dr. Emma Parker. If it's an emergency, please hang up and dial 9-1-1. Otherwise, leave me a message."

"Hey, baby. I just got your message. Give me a call back when you get this. It's important. I love you," I say and then disconnect. And I do it with a sinking feeling in my gut.

What is mitochondrial DNA? I have to find out. This feels like the break in the case I've been waiting for. But... what does it have to do with Emma's ex, Jerrod? I do not like that he's involved in this in any way.

I hit Redial on my phone and lift it back to my ear. I have to talk to Emma. Something doesn't feel right here, and I've been gone way too long. I should have been home hours ago.

It rings and rings, and then, "You've reached Dr. Emma Parker...."

"God dammit," I bite out.

Why isn't she answering her phone?

"Hey, baby, it's me again. Call me as soon as you get this? Humor a nervous soon-to-be dad, okay?"

And then I hang up.

I need to find out about this DNA thing and fast, and I need to get to Emma.

"Is everything all right?" my dad asks. I didn't notice his approach, so he took me by surprise.

I look up at him, and I can tell he sees the answer written across my face, but I reply anyway, "I don't think so."

"What can I do to help?"

"Do you know anything about mitochondrial DNA?" I ask. My dad had my job when Claire and I were kids. He went on to be Chief of Police for the township. He's one of the best police officers I've ever known, so the question isn't for nothing.

"I'm sorry, son," he says, and I can tell by his tone that he really means it. "What do you need to know for?"

"It has to do with a case I'm working," I answer him. "Emma left me a message while I was deeper in the hospital with no service, saying there was a mitochondrial match to the first victim, a Jane Doe, but now

Emma's not answering, and I need to know."

"I think I can help you," the sweet nurse who came to Wes to tell him Claire was going to be all right says. "You're asking about mitochondrial DNA?"

"Yeah," I reply. "What can you tell me about it?"

"Mitochondrial DNA is like a little circular ring of DNA found in the mitochondria," she says, smiling kindly.

"And this is important?" I ask.

"It is, because it comes almost exclusively from your mama," she explains. "So if you have a mitochondrial match, that would be a mother and her child kind of match."

Holy fuck.

A mother and her child kind of match.

Emma's douchey ex is the son of my killer.

"Did that help?" she asks, looking a little unsure.

"More than you could ever know," I answer, dropping a quick kiss to her cheek before turning to my dad. "I gotta go. Call dispatch and send them to my house."

"Why?" he asks, suddenly alert. It wasn't too long ago that he was shot and almost died trying to rescue my sister. To Dad, family is everything.

"Just a gut reaction," I answer immediately.

"And you think Emma is in trouble?"

"Yes," I answer him without hesitation.

"Then you better get moving," he says. "I'll call dispatch."

"Thanks, Dad."

"I love you, Lee," he says as he pulls his phone out of his pocket and starts dialing a familiar number.

"I love you too," I tell him as I turn and head out of the hospital.

I unlock my phone and hit the Redial button again. It rings and rings.

"Come on, Emma. Pick up."

And then, "You've reached Dr. Emma Parker...."

"Fuck!" I bite out. "Goddammit, Emma. Answer the phone."

I hang up and pull my keys from my pocket, realizing my car is still at Imperial Dragons, so I race back into the hospital. Dad sees me immediately.

"Lee? What are you doing back?"

"My car is still at the restaurant," I answer. "I rode here with Claire in the ambulance."

"Here," he says, pulling his keys from his pocket and tossing them to me. "I'm right out front in the ER lot."

"Thanks, Dad."

"Don't worry about it," he says. "Go get your girl. I'll get a cab to your car."

"Thanks," I say, tossing him my keys, and then I'm running through the big sliding glass doors that do not open fast enough for my liking.

Dad's gray Expedition is right where he said it would be. Last year, when he and Mom gained custody of my older sister's kids, he promptly traded in the BMW he had always wanted for a big soccer mom SUV. He drives Seth and all his friends to baseball practices and soccer games, and he loves every minute of it.

I beep the locks on it and climb in. I set my phone on the dash while I buckle up and back out of the space. Once I'm on the road, I pick it up again and dial. It rings and rings, and then, *"You've reached Dr. Emma Parker. If it's an emergency, please hang up and dial 9-1-1. Otherwise, leave me a message."*

I slap the steering wheel. Fuck!

"Hey, Emma, it's me. I really need you to call me. And don't answer the door to anyone who is not me. But I really need you to call me."

And then I hang up and drive like a bat out of hell.

And it's really too bad that even though this is a fairly small township and the drive is not long at all, I still wouldn't make it in time.

twenty-two

betrayed
EMMA

Forty-five minutes earlier

hips or cookies? Chips or cookies? I vacillate between the two basic snack groups while staring through the open door to the pantry.

Maybe an apple? Yeah, no. Probably not.

Cookies or chips?

I reach for the brand-new bag of Cape Cod Salt and Vinegar Kettle Chips, a staple that saw me through most of this pregnancy and my heartbreak emotional eating when I thought I couldn't have my happily ever after with Lee. What a funny, girly saying, "happily ever after." It was so Anna and all of her romantic dreams, not only for herself but those around her.

And for the first time in almost a year, it doesn't

hurt nearly as much to think of my fallen friend.

I see now she was not perfect, that she made mistakes that were also selfish choices that hurt not only herself but those around her. But with all of that, it also does not mean she was a bad person or a shitty friend. She was awesome, and we loved her as much as she loved us. So now I see Claire was right when she yelled at me and told me that avoiding Lee and denying what was growing between us was not what she would have wanted. In fact, her dying words were for us to turn to each other, to love each other, and I denied her last request for almost a year.

But I was done with that. Now, I was going to move forward the only way I knew how—as me. And I'm a person who no longer wants to live her life bogged down by the ugly that life has dealt. I want to show the sweet little girl growing inside me that life is beautiful, and I want to do that with her daddy at my side, because now I know without a doubt that with him, life *is* beautiful. I want to give him three more beautiful, perfect babies and grow old with him and watch our four babies grow into decent human beings. I want to marry him and celebrate anniversaries with him.

And most of all, I want to love him and be loved by him and only him.

It's with that thought and a smile on my face that I pick up my ringing cell phone from the island countertop and slide my finger across the screen to answer it.

"Dr. Emma Parker, how may I help you?"

"Hello, Dr. Parker, this is Dr. Javier Martinez with the state crime lab," the caller identifies themselves. And hopefully they have some results for me, because I know Lee is getting frustrated with the current state of play with the baby-snatcher case. And I get it, I really do. I hate how many women have been murdered in such a short period of time and their babies just… gone. I don't even want to imagine what those shoes feel like.

"It's good to hear from you, Dr. Martinez," I answer. "I'm hoping you have news for me."

"I do. Is now a good time to discuss those finding with you?"

"It is." I grab a pen and a tablet and haul my big ass up onto one of the barstools and settle in. I know I'm not really big, but I'm into the final trimester of baby cooking, and apparently with that comes huge body changes, and I mean huge.

"Excellent," he agrees. "I have already faxed the official reports to your office, but I wanted to be able to go over them with you on the phone before you hit your desk Monday morning."

"I'm actually home on an emergency medical leave," I explain. "So I'm glad you phoned."

"I'm sorry to hear that. I hope all is well," he mumbles.

"It is now."

"Great news," he says awkwardly. I find that doctors like us who spend more time with the dead than the living don't often have the best social skills, but whatever. It is what it is.

"So about those findings," I prompt, bailing him out. I know he appreciates it, when I hear his relieved sigh.

"Yes," he says, pressing on. "But not with the victims, per se. I found a mitochondrial DNA match."

"To who?" I'm practically salivating, waiting for the answer. This is a huge break in the case. Whatever match he found, someone is connected to the killings in some way. I just hope his results can explain how.

"The defensive wound skin and blood you collected from under Jane Doe's fingernails at the original scene," Dr. Martinez answers me.

Oh my God. This is huge.

"What collection finally matched?" I ask. "I'm sorry I'm not following along."

"That's quite all right," he replies. "I find I've gotten ahead of myself in my enthusiasm."

"That's okay. I'm excited by this development too."

"The skin and blood collected from under Jane Doe's fingernails is a mitochondrial match to the hair sample you sent after the last scene."

The hair.

The hair Lee said was found and bagged randomly after the entire scene was combed through by not only his team but mine. This means Lee knows something that I do not. I need to call him with this information right away.

"Thank you so much," I tell him. "I look forward to reading your complete findings Monday morning."

"Of course."

"You'll forgive me if I need to let you go to pass this information on to the lead officer on the investigation?" I ask.

"Of course," he repeats instantly. "Have a good day, Dr. Parker."

"Same to you, Dr. Martinez," I reply before I press the button to disconnect the call.

I don't set my phone down even for a second. I don't know what it is, but I have a feeling these findings are huge, huge in the sense that they could break Lee's case wide open and maybe save some poor woman's life.

God, I hope so. I can't imagine being cut open alive like that.

A violent shudder wracks up my spine, and I press the button to call Lee. It rings and rings, and then, "You've reached Captain Liam Goodnite with the George Washington Township Police Department. If this is an emergency, please hang up and dial 9-1-1. If it is not an emergency, please leave a message at the tone, and I will get back to you as soon as I can."

I press the red circle button to hang up and then set my phone on the kitchen counter.

"Shit," I mumble as soon as I hang up. Where is he?

Why isn't he answering? They're just at lunch, right?

I pick up my phone and dial again. "You've reached Captain Liam Goodnite…"

This time, without taking a breath, I launch into my nervous explanation as soon as I hear the beep. "Hey, honey, it's me. I know you're out with your sister, but I haven't heard from you in a while. I hope everything is okay. Anyway, that's not why I'm calling. I just got off the phone with the state lab, and they said the hair you found at the crime scene is a mitochondrial match to the defensive wound DNA found under Jane Doe's fingernails. Anyways, let me know if you'll be home for dinner. I'm feeling like pizza. Shocking, right? I love you, Lee."

I press the button to disconnect again, and my belly lets out a loud rumble, reminding me that I was looking for a snack before Dr. Martinez phoned. I push out a heavy breath and try to force the tension out of my shoulder muscles. I roll my neck from side to side in order to work out some kinks and make my way back to the pantry, where I grab the bag of chips from the shelf and pull it open. I reach inside and pluck one out, and I'm just about to pop the whole thing in my mouth, when the doorbell rings.

"You have got to be kidding me." I sigh as I drop the chip back in the bag. Gross, I know, but it's not really, because I know I'm going to eat the entire bag, so it's not like I have to worry about someone else, mainly Lee, picking up my cross contamination. And besides that, he likes to put his tongue in my mouth as well as other places, so I feel the point is really moot.

I set the bag of chips on the counter near my cell phone and make my way to the front door to answer it. This would be my third mistake of the day behind not going to lunch with Claire and Lee, the first mistake I made, as it would have taken me from this moment here, and the second being only moments ago, when I left my phone on the kitchen counter and out of reach.

Of course, I didn't know that all three of those mistakes added up to one big, deadly clusterfuck until right now.

So, not looking through the front window to see who would darken Lee's door in the late afternoon or early evening of a weekend day, instead, I pull open the door like a moron. And then I stand there, staring with my mouth hanging open and huge eyes at who is on the front porch.

"Jerrod?" I ask stupidly, because who else would he be?

And then he put a hand to my burgeoning belly and pushed me back into the house, following in behind me. I should have noticed now, but I was too distracted by his suddenly being at Lee's house when I had not seen him in a while. Later, I would realize that he shut the front door, but he did not lock it.

"What are you doing here?"

"I told you," he says, panicked. I don't like the look on his face, but he's tweaked about something, and it's not okay. "I tried to warn you, and now it's too late."

"Jerrod?" I whisper. "You're scaring me. What's too late?"

"You should have chosen me," he snaps. "I could have saved you."

"W-w-what are you talking about?" I don't like the look in his eye. How did I miss that he was absolutely batshit crazy?

"If you'd have only agreed to give up the baby, we could be together," he says as he crowds me in. Jerrod is so close I'm not sure I could get around him.

"Jerrod," I say carefully. "You know she's not your child."

"But I loved you!" he screams. "I could have saved you!"

"Saved me from what exactly?" I ask, knowing damn well I probably don't want to know the answer to my question.

I hear my phone ringing in the kitchen, and I look that way, but he places his hand on my face and not in a good way, shoving me back so I'm forced to look at his madness shining in his eyes.

"I could have saved you," he repeats strongly, and I can't look away from the wrongness on his face and in his eyes. "But now you have to die."

"No," I whisper. "You don't mean that."

But the grip he has on my face turns harsher, his fingers biting into the flesh of my face.

My phone stops ringing only to start up again.

"We can get past this," I hedge. I need to get him to let me go. I work for law enforcement, and with that, it entitles me to concealed carry for my protection. I have been trained in guns for professional use, and I keep that certification current. And if I can get past him, I can get to one of the safes Lee has in this house and get to a gun. I have to.

I have to protect myself and, with that, my baby.

"There's nothing to talk about," he says, and I realize then that his voice sounds dead. It ratchets up the panic that's soaring through my body.

My phone rings again, but I don't make the mistake of looking at it this time, not only because I don't want to enrage him more, but because I'm realizing now that not only shouldn't I have answered the door, I should have paid attention, because when he shut it behind himself, he didn't lock it, as it creaks when it's pushed open again. I then realize the monster I let into this house has let in a bigger one.

"Hello, Dr. Parker," Madame Driskill says, her cruel, smiling eyes alight with the terror she's about to inflict. "So we meet again."

"W-w-what are you doing here?" I whisper. I can barely get the words pushed out of my mouth, because I know in my heart that whatever reason they are here for is not only not good; it's dangerous.

"I believe my son warned you that there would be consequences for denying him," she says with a vicious smile.

I don't respond, I'm not even sure how I could without escalating things further, and then the meaning of her words slams into my brain like a freight train.

"What do you mean?" I ask hesitantly. "Your son?"

"Just that," she answers. "Jerrod is my child. I guess you could say we work together."

"At the adoption agency?" I prompt before looking back to the man I had once considered trying something with and for whatever reason could never pull the trigger. "I thought you were in IT?"

"Something like that," he mumbles, and she lets out a trilling laugh.

"IT?" she asks, still finding something humorous, but what, I do not know. "That's funny."

"Why?" I snap, suddenly becoming angry. "Why is it funny?"

"I guess you could consider my son a problem solver of sorts, but it has nothing to do with technology," she answers with a cat who got their cream smile that I do not like at all.

"What do you mean?" In the background, I hear my phone ringing again before it stops.

"Do you really want all the dirty details?" she asks me. "Isn't it sometimes better not to know?"

"No," I answer immediately. "I think I have the right to know why—that is, if I'm about to die."

"Oh, you most certainly are," she says, and she has the audacity to wink at me, and it takes every last inch of my control not to lose my damn mind. "But I guess I can honor your wishes, since you are a very special case."

"Thank you." I don't mean it, but I have to keep her talking. My only hope now is that Lee got my message, and when he can't get a hold of me, he'll head straight home. Until then, I know I need to keep them talking. The longer they talk, the longer it will take them to kill me.

"It all started with the adoption agency," she says.

"So it's real?"

"Of course it's real," she answers, and her friendly nature is nothing but false. I can see her true malice burning in her eyes. "I can see how you'd think it wasn't. We really do run private adoptions to very wealthy but also tragically infertile clientele. I like to think that every baby deserves a loving home."

"Then why not adopt out unwanted babies?" I ask. "Why bother taking the ones who are wanted?"

"That's a two-parter question," she replies. "First, we do adopt out the unwanted, but it's the babies of higher caliber that bring in more money. Your baby, for example, has already sold for five hundred thousand dollars. The fact that he comes from an intelligent doctor is apparently rather appealing."

"The baby isn't a boy; it's a girl," I correct her.

"Well, that's a disappointment," she says. "Although, I'm sure I can talk them into keeping the original price. Most people want boys, but your daughter would be beautiful too."

"Thank you, I think."

"Oh, I meant it as a compliment."

"And Jerrod, if that is even his name?" I ask.

"Oh it is, but our surnames are fictitious," she says. "You understand why?"

"I do."

My phone rings again, and I hope they don't notice it.

"He steps in on difficult cases," she answers. "Like yourself."

"Why was I a difficult case?" I ask. "I was never giving up my baby."

"That's why you were difficult," she explains. "If you'd have just signed the adoption contract, this all would be ending differently. But you didn't, and I wanted your baby."

"But why?"

"Because she's worthy enough to sell for a lot of money," she snaps before righting her composure. "We've already been over this."

"And what happens to mothers who sign your contract and then back out?" I ask, even though I know again that it's an answer to a question I don't want to learn.

"They die just like you're about to."

"And Jerrod?"

"He gets close to the target and convinces them to change their mind." She rolls her eyes at me like I'm an idiot. Which, arguably, I am, because I managed to let these two monsters into my life. "Although, you're the first one he asked me to keep."

I can't help the shudder that wracks up my body at the thought of him "wanting to keep" me. Jerrod shoots me an angry glare, but his mother smiles wider at me.

"And now you know," she says. "And it's time to move on."

"No!" I shout, but I don't even get the chance to struggle, because she strikes out like a snake. I hadn't even noticed the injector pen in her hand until it was too late. "You won't get away with this."

"I'm afraid I already have," she replies with a mean smile as I feel my legs begin to give out, and Jerrod lays me down on the floor of the living room.

"No," I reply, but I have to lick my lips. They're dry; my mouth is so dry. It feels like I'll never not be thirsty again, but I have to push past it. "Lee got a hair sample from Jerrod at one of the crime scenes. It was a mitochondrial match to the skin and blood found under the fingernails of a Jane Doe.

"No," she snaps, her eyes shooting fire at her son.

"Yes," I answer. "I already told Lee, and the results from the state lab are in my office."

My body flushes hot, too, too hot. I'm burning up. I'm on fire.

"You stupid fool!" she screams. "I can't believe you let your cock ruin my plan. It was perfect!"

"We can still win, Mother," he says. "There's still time."

"Yes," she says coolly. "There's still time."

And then she pulls a small gun from her pocket and shoots her son dead.

I flit my eyes around, but my mouth won't work anymore. I want to scream, but I can't. Oh my God. There is no one left to save me. I can only pray now that my baby lives a happy life. That's all I ever wanted.

I feel a tear slide down my cheek and into my hair. It's weird. It's like it's there but not. No doubt the effects of atropine poisoning. I watch as she slips out several baby blankets and lays them on top of the small duffle bag she was carrying. And then she pulls a scalpel from a small protective sheath. It gleams in the lights of the room.

"Don't worry," she says. "You shouldn't feel a thing."

And then I watch helplessly as she places the tip of the scalpel to my skin and slowly draws an evil smile. I want to watch my child be born, but as my blood starts to bead up and then roll down one by one, I start to feel a little fuzzy. I don't know whether to hang on and fight or drift off into painless oblivion.

I gasp, my breaths coming faster and faster as she rocks and pulls at my body to wiggle my tiny baby out.

"Emma!" we both hear Lee shout. "Emma! Are you in there?"

"If you know what's good for you, you'll keep your mouth shut," she whispers harshly, and it doesn't matter, because I can't. My mouth is frozen, and my voice is nowhere to be found.

She pulls harder and faster at my body again and again, and then I feel a sense of being… empty.

I'm empty. There is nothing left to me, and as I watch Madame Driskill pull my tiny baby all covered in goo up and wraps her in the pink baby blankets as the room turns to mist and swirls all around me.

I hear Lee's key in the lock and sirens in the distance.

And then she scoops up my baby and races up the stairs just before the front door bursts open and Lee is there. Thank God, he's there.

I open my mouth to tell him that he needs to save her. He has to save our daughter. But I'm not sure if I get the words out, because the lights dim to black.

And then I die.

I am no more.

I'm just… empty.

twenty-three

everything i ever wanted
LIAM

I stomp my foot down on the gas and flip on the lights and sirens as I race back to Emma and hope I'm not too late.

Please, God, don't let me be too late.

And I cannot fucking believe it was that sick fuck the whole fucking time. I am so fucking stupid. I was so blinded by my jealousy and so deep in my own misery that I didn't push it. I knew there was something off about him, but I chalked it up to him getting the girl that I was totally and hopelessly gone for. Nothing more.

But it was so fucking much more. I should have seen it was so much more.

And I call. The whole time I drive, I dial her number over and over. And every time, it rings and rings, and then I get her voicemail message. Again. I don't bother leaving messages anymore; I just hang up and dial again. And again and again. But still nothing.

Finally, I pull into the driveway and throw my truck in park before I'm leaping from the vehicle and shouting down the neighborhood while I race up the lawn and straight to the front door.

"Emma!" I shout as I struggle to get my dad's keys to separate, my fingers shaking so bad. Thank God I gave my dad a key to my house. "Emma! Are you in there?"

And then I finally get the front door open, and the first thing I notice is... *blood.*

There's so much fucking blood. The stuff is everywhere. Dark-red and sticky, it seeps down like fingers reaching for more. It's like a monster in the night seeking another victim. I haven't seen this much blood and carnage since the last time I was in the desert.

Hell, even Anna's death wasn't this gruesome.

I rush toward her and drop to my knees. I need to staunch the flow, but there is so much. I'm not sure where to start or how. I pull my cell phone out of my pants pocket and dial dispatch.

"9-1-1, what is the nature of your emergency?" the dispatcher answers. I don't have time to listen for who it is.

Christ. Jesus Fucking Christ, don't let her be dead.

"This is Captain Goodnite, and I need an ambulance at 1431 Poinsettia Drive," I bark into my phone.

"It's an emergency."

She's not dead yet. Her eyes blink open at the sound of my voice and then flit around wildly. There is a shock to this kind of trauma. I have seen men on the battlefield not realize they were mortally wounded or missing limbs. *Please don't let her fucking die.*

"Hang in there," I command her and hope to fuck that for once in her life she listens to me. "It's going to be okay." I just hope I can back up those claims.

Today was supposed to be such a simple day. Lunch with my sister so she doesn't drive her husband to homicide and then a quiet dinner at home with my girl. When Claire's contractions at the restaurant ended in an ambulance ride and emergency surgery, I should have known better.

I spent the afternoon and earlier part of the evening at the hospital. Until I had this weird feeling something was wrong. It's been a long fucking time since I had a gut check. Those instincts saved me more than a few times on missions. Finally, when I could barely stand it, Wes gave me the all-clear on my sister and her kids, so I rushed home.

Fuck me. There's so much blood. My heart pounds in my chest, and I swallow back against the desert that has invaded my mouth. She's still bleeding. I have to stop the bleeding. I cross my arms over my abs and whip my T-shirt over my head. I press it to the wound that gapes open like a gruesome smile. *They didn't even try to stitch her up.*

Her blood is wicking up through my shirt by the time I see the blue-and-red lights flashing on the wall of my living room. She should have been sitting on the sofa in her sweatpants and watching *The Real Housewives* of Something Stupid. She loves those dumb fucking reality shows almost as much as I love to tease her about them.

There's a knock at the door. Thank Christ.

"We're in here," I call out.

"What do we have?" one of the paramedics asks me as they roll in a gurney.

"Another baby-snatcher victim," I answer.

"Then you need the ME, not us," his partner says.

"This is the medical examiner," I inform them. "And she's still alive."

"Fuck," one of them bites out.

"L-Lee," she rasps and licks her dry lips. Her beautiful blue eyes blink and flit all around.

"I'm right here, baby," I say as I hold her hand in mine.

"I-i-it was—" she starts before her eyes roll back in her head and her whole body begins to shake.

"She's coding!" one of the paramedics shouts.

"Sir!" the other one barks at me as he tries to push me away from her body. "Sir, you have to get back."

I scoot back a foot or two so they can work, and I draw my knees up to my chest. I feel a hand on my shoulder and look up into the understanding eyes of Detective Jones. He thinks she's going to die, but I haven't come this far to give up now.

She can't die on me. I just got her back in my life, got to feel the warmth of her skin pressed against mine, the sounds of her laughter, the sight of her in my house, and the dreams of a future. A future that, as I take in the scene around me, is starting to go missing.

As they work on Emma and prepare her to transport to the hospital, their voices carry as the two paramedics shout to each other what they need to keep her breathing. It's faint at first. Somewhere deep in the back of my house, I hear a baby cry.

"Captain!" Jones shouts as I jump up.

Christ. Fucking Christ. She's still here. The baby is still here.

I reach for my ankle holster and slip my drop gun free. I hold it loose at my side as I race up the stairs. There's not much but the kitchen and laundry room at the back of the first floor, so I know she has to be hiding with the baby—*my baby*—up here.

I clear doorways, one by one, just like we were taught so many years ago in the navy. That SEAL training never really leaves you, especially when it's compounded with police training.

My office is empty and dark.

Same with our bedroom and the bathroom off the hall.

She wouldn't.

It can't be.

But as I push open the door to the room that Wes and I worked our asses off to transform into Emma's dream nursery for her baby, the perfect room for my princess, I see it's exactly that. It's my worst nightmare. A wolf in sheep's clothing is sitting in the rocker I bought for my woman to rock our child in, and she's holding a very tiny bundle wrapped up in pink blankets. But this baby was born too soon and will likely need medical attention as well. I need to get to her and fast. But I still have to be careful.

"Hello, Captain Goodnite," the older woman greets me, and I realize she's the woman who ran the adoption agency, the same one who was pressing Emma to give up her baby. The very same one Emma's ex was trying to strong arm her into giving the baby to.

"Hello, Madame Driskill," I say coolly. "Please hand over my daughter."

"Not so fast," she says as she raises a gun when I take a step toward where she sits holding my baby.

"You can go," I lie to her. "Just hand me my daughter and walk out of this room."

"She won't survive, you know," she says casually. "They all die."

"Like your son?" I ask, hoping I can distract her, but she still aims her gun at my child. I raise mine to her, and we take our places in a terrifying standoff.

"He made a stupid mistake."

"And that mistake will cost you."

"It already has," she snaps. "Do you think I'm going to get out of here alive?"

"You can," I tell her. She might get the gas chamber once a jury gets wind of all she's done, but I'm not going to mention that right now. "Just don't take my daughter with you."

"I should," she says, and I feel my whole body go still. "You deserve it for ruining my entire operation. But now, Captain Goodnite, you have to make a choice."

"What choice?" I bite out. I'm barely breathing, barely hanging on. Emma is downstairs fighting for her life, and one false move and this monster will take my child too.

"You could shoot me or…" she trails off. She's baiting me into having this insane conversation, and we both know it.

"Or what?"

"Catch," she says, and then my heart stops fucking beating as she tosses the tiny bundle of pink blankets that is my daughter high up into the air so that I have to drop my weapon in order to catch her, and I do not even hesitate for one fucking second before I let my gun clatter to the floor, hoping against all fucking hope that this isn't a trap to kill us both.

I watch helplessly as the woman raises the gun to

her temple when I leap for the tiny bundle. She winks at me with a smile on her face.

"It was a good run." And then she pulls the trigger.

The gunshot echoes through the room.

Jones and other officers storm upstairs and take in the scene.

"It's over," he says to me, but I just nod and then run out of the room, because I have to get to Emma.

I race down the stairs and catch the paramedics as they load her up into the back of the ambulance, and I jump in after her with our baby in my arms, taking both paramedics by surprise.

"Let's go!" the one in the back shouts to the driver as he slams the doors closed on us, and I hand over my most precious bundle for him to look over.

He cleans her up and suctions her mouth and nose, but her color looks good and she's breathing on her own. That's about all I remember from the last baby I delivered while on duty.

"She looks good," he whispers before handing her back to me to hold. I don't know if it's because he sees I'm hanging on to my last fucking thread or because he needs to keep an eye on Emma, or maybe even a little bit of both. I'm just glad to have her back in my arms. "We'll have her looked over at the hospital."

"Thank you."

He just nods, and we sit in silence and listen to the beeps of the monitor as we ride to the hospital. And once we arrive, Emma is whisked into the operating room, and I don't even get the chance to kiss her one last time.

I hope it's not goodbye.

And the baby and I are escorted to the neonatal intensive care unit, where the attending pediatrician comes in, looking a little shell-shocked. Her face is pale in contrast to her pink scrubs with smiley faces all over them. Someone must have briefed her on the nature of this child's delivery into the world.

The windows Lee and I stood at earlier are once again covered so that just anyone can't see in. The room is empty other than the two nurses looking after the little bundles in the corner, one pink and one blue; otherwise, all of the little glass bassinets are empty. Those must be my sister's kids.

"She looks good, but we're going to need to keep her for observation just to make sure her little lungs are up to speed," the doctor says to me. "I'm going to give her a steroid shot that will boost them up a bit more."

"Okay," I say, but I mean, what else can I do? I'm just so fucking helpless.

"There are only two other babies here right now," she says. "So she'll have our mostly undivided attention."

"Are those the O'Connell twins?" I ask as I look back to the pink and blue bundles.

"Yes," she says, tipping her head to the side in an attractive manner as she eyes me. "How did you know?"

"Their mom is my sister," I answer.

"Three babies in one day," she says surprised. "What a big day for your parents, who I've had the pleasure of meeting."

"I was wondering…" I trail off.

"Yes?"

"Could she… the baby I mean… be with her cousins when I can't be with her?" I ask. "I want her to be near family."

"I think that sounds fair, since they all had such a harrowing day," she says. "Now, we do need you out for a bit. Visiting hours resume in two hours here in the NICU, or we can have her brought to you when you're settled. That reminds me, did you all have a name for her?"

"I… uhh… we—" I stammer, and she must see the pain and fear etched across my face, because she interrupts quickly.

"I'm so sorry. I shouldn't have asked."

"It's fine."

"It's not, but it will be," she assures. "And besides, there's no rush on these things. You have plenty of time to decide on a name."

"I wanted…" I have to clear my throat to get the words out. "I want her mom and me to decide together."

"That's lovely," she says.

"I should go see if my family is still around."

"They are, and I've been told they're waiting for you," she informs me. "She'll be in good hands. You have my promise."

"Thank you."

And then I walk out of the NICU and back to the waiting room to wait for news on Emma with my family. Everyone is still there. Even Wes makes an appearance when he hears I'm back.

But it isn't until my dad folds me into his arms that I fucking lose it, and I cry like a little baby, because Emma is everything I ever wanted, and if I lose her and our baby, what do I have left?

Eyes.

The smell of sulfur fills my nostrils, and smoke sears my lungs. The heavy weight of the rifle in my hands is like second nature to me. I could carry it in my sleep. During training, I probably did.

But it's the eyes that chill me to the bone in the middle of this hot desert.

I don't know how the intel had gone so bad. I know it happens, but not like this. One minute, the mission was going to plan, and the next, the world exploded. Spurts of gunfire can be heard all around me, but it's the screams that ring in my ears.

"Fuck, fuck, fuck!" I hear Adams scream through

the comms in my ear. "They're dead. They're all dead."

And he's right. They're all dead. Every last one of them. I was helpless to prevent this, and still I feel like I should have. It's as bad is if their blood were directly on my hands.

I make my way through the village we've been watching, my heart in my throat. Buildings, homes, the carts in the market, they're all gone, burned-out shells of what they were before. And bodies crumpled where they fell. Men, women, children—death does not discriminate. Their eyes are vacant after life left them.

If eyes are the windows to the soul, then this is a portal to hell as I look at the faces of each person who should not have died. A child we gave a candy bar to yesterday, an old lady who offered coffee in the market, and a beautiful young woman whose belly was swollen with a baby.

Her dark eyes watch me, haunt me, as she sees me and nothing at all. And then they change to Emma's blue ones, her belly cut open, and our baby is just... gone.

The smoke burns my throat as I see Emma's blonde-and-pink hair, her blue eyes open and watching me, her beautiful body mutilated, because I was in her life.

"No!" I shout.

But the eyes of the dead scream that this is all my fault.

I should have known.

This is all my fault.

And now she's dead too.

My breath seizes in my lungs as I come awake with a start.

It was just a dream, a bad dream. A horrible fucking dream. One that I think will be with me for the rest of my life.

I sit up in my chair, and once again, I watch Emma sleeping in a hospital bed. The moon glows through the slats of the blinds in the window and casts an ethereal glimmer on her pale skin.

She's too fucking pale, probably because she lost too much blood. They told me it took three transfusions to put her back together again. And the worst part of all, that bitch robbed Emma of her ability to have more children. We're too new to have talked about baby names and for the majority of the time, I didn't know that she was mine and I got a vote. Baby Girl Goodnite, as the sign on her hospital bassinet proclaims for now, but I would've at least liked the opportunity to have a fucking conversation.

Four. I can't stop thinking that she wanted four children, three more after this baby. And I would have happily given her everyone of them that she wanted. I'd will it to be two boys and another girl just like she wanted. That choice should be Emma's, not decided by anyone else, and she took that from us.

I don't go back to sleep. I sit and seethe. I nurse my anger while I listen to the beeps that tell me my woman is still breathing. And I do it thinking that if the bitch weren't already dead, I'd gladly kill her.

But that's another thing she stole from us—my ability to put her down. Then again, I guess that would not bode well for my future in law enforcement or look good in the fact that a friend of mine somehow managed to get elected to the White House. These are wild times. So I guess it's best after all that I didn't get to kill her.

I still don't sleep.

I sit and watch Emma. I watch the seconds turn to minutes that turn to hours on the clock. But I don't go to sleep.

And then, finally, fucking finally, sometime after the sun rose up in the sky, the most beautiful blue eyes I've ever seen flutter open and look right at me. And then her whole face crumples and she begins to cry.

"Honey, what's wrong?" I ask softly and then mentally kick myself, because what didn't go fucking wrong yesterday?

"You saved me," she sobs quietly.

"I'm so sorry I wasn't there for you," I whisper as I gently brush her hair back from her face. "I'm so fucking sorry." I say it over and over again until she gets it, until she feels it down deep like I do.

"You came for me." She sniffles. "You saved me."

"Yeah."

"Thank you."

"It's over, Emma. You're safe. The baby is safe. It's over."

"It's over," she repeats, but she doesn't stop crying.

"Honey, talk to me," I beg. "Tell me what to do."

"They told me," she whispers.

"What, baby? Tell me what they told you."

"You know what the last thought I had was before I opened the door?" she asks, and I'm not following where this jump is going. Maybe she's still groggy.

"I don't know, baby. What did you think?" I ask, and as soon as she answers, I wish I could rewind the clock and go back five minutes and never ask it. That's how deeply I feel the pain she's feeling.

"That I was going to marry you and give you three more babies after this one," she says. "That I was going to fill your house with love and happy babies and give you back as much of the sweet that you gave me."

"Emma—" I start, and it comes out pained. She knows, and I know, and we both know that the other knows, and it fucking kills.

"But I can't do that," she continues. "I can't give you that sweet. I'm broken."

"You're not fucking broken," I bark, and she startles a bit, so I gentle my voice when I continue. "You are not broken. You cannot carry more children, because they had to take your uterus, and honey, that pains me to have to fucking give you that. It kills me to know they robbed you of that. But you are not broken. You're a survivor. And we're going to get through this together, because we're not going to go it apart ever again. I can't go through that again. All right?"

"All right, Lee," she whispers.

"And if you want more babies after this one—which we still have to name, by the way—then we'll adopt all the babies we can who need a safe place to land. Or if you want some of our own blood, then we'll hire a surrogate to carry, because we can still do that. And it'll cost a whack, but I figure Wes is sitting on top of all those piles of blood money from his dickhead relatives—may they rot in hell—so he'd be happy to cut some checks for some fancy surrogates."

"Okay, Lee," she says, but this time there's a little bit of a twinkle in her eyes.

"And baby, you've gotta know."

"Know what?" she prompts quietly.

"That if I have you, I already have everything I ever wanted," I tell her, and the hitch in her breath and the water pooling in her eyes tell me that I'm everything she's ever wanted too. "So let's get you well and then figure out the rest together. Deal?"

"Deal."

epilogue

ties that bind

Six weeks later

As carefully as I can, I lift up the covers and slide out from underneath Emma's arm. She's still sound asleep, and I know she could use more rest, so I'm going to try not to wake her.

"Shh, baby girl," I whisper with a smile for the most beautiful baby I've ever seen in my life. "Let's let Mommy sleep."

Hope just smiles her squishy baby smile for me, and I scoop her up out of her bassinet, carrying her out of our room and down the hall to her room. The first time Hope and I were in this room together, it was transformed from a dream nursery into a nightmare, and now, you would never know. While Emma was recovering in the hospital, my parents and a bunch of guys from the station scrubbed this room within an inch of its life, and they started the second the crime scene tape came down. My mother and grandmother, I was told much later, ruthlessly tossed anything that couldn't be salvaged, and everything that was tossed was replaced with brand-new.

It looks exactly like what Wes and I built for my girls, and this is how I will always see it. I'm trying my best not to give too much headspace to all that's happened and all we've lost. At least not yet. I know we're going to have to work through a lot, but until then, I just want to soak in this little bit of happy first.

So I change diapers like the one I just changed and put my girl in pink ruffle jammies, because she deserves to live in a world where such things exist and no bad can ever touch her ever again. She begins to fuss a bit as I carry her against my shoulder down to the kitchen to fix her a bottle, but my girl is not a crier. She might fuss a bit, but for the most part, she's just a happy baby. That might change in the future, but I don't care. I love every minute I've been given with these two women, and I swear to God I will not waste a moment of it. It's all too precious.

I carry her and her bottle back to her room, because I like to be close to Emma, even when I'm trying to give her space to sleep. I'm not ready to be apart from her just yet. So we're all back upstairs, but Hope and I are in the nursery, and we settle into the big chair that's a replica of the one I chose for Emma.

I curl my girl into the crook of my arm, and she smiles at me. I smile right back as the bottle slips into her mouth and she eats her early-morning meal while we watch the sun come up in New Jersey. And just like that sunrise, just like every time I look at her face, I feel nothing but hope for the future. Emma wanted to honor Anna in a way that she would continue to live on with us—no longer between us, but a part of our family—and there was no better way to watch her live on than through our daughter. So it was decided, and Hope Anne was written on a birth certificate that we had to jump through some hoops and tear down some red tape to get, because the birth attendant was dead and there was no one to answer any questions. But I still made it happen. I would do anything for my girls.

"Hey," Emma says from the doorway, and she looks so fucking beautiful. She takes my breath away every time I look at her. "There you guys are."

"We wanted to let you get some sleep."

"Who needs sleep when I have you guys?" she asks cheekily, and I'm reminded that through it all, I got everything I ever wanted, and the proposal I've been planning for near on two months goes right out the window.

"Marry me," I tell her softly, my voice a little gruff with emotion.

"What?" She laughs as her eyes snap from our daughter to mine.

"You heard me," I say, letting my voice ring strong and true this time. "I asked you to marry me, because honey, I have been tied up in your strings since the moment you opened my eyes to all that was you and everything I ever wanted, and I never want to be un-tangled. I want to grow old with you and watch this girl grow up, and I want you to yell at me when I scare off all her boyfriends, when really it makes you happy, be-cause you know 'the one' won't back down in the face of a protective father. 'The one' will walk through hell and still press on to deserve a life of beauty with our daughter. I want to give you your own life of beauty, even if that means I have to walk through hell again and again to prove I'm worthy to give it to you. Until the day I die. The rest of my life will never be enough, but I'll take it and be grateful, because it was with you. So, baby, I'm asking you to marry me."

"Yes," she whispers as tears stream down her face, but her smile is blinding, so I know they are happy tears, something new to add to my Emma with post-pregnancy hormones, and I love this softer side of her. I also love that she's a badass. It's called balance.

"Top drawer. In the back."

"What?" she asks at my sudden change of pace.

"Because my hands are a little full right now," I say, nodding toward the now sleeping baby in my lap. "I need you to look in the back of the top drawer."

And I watch, my heart beating faster as she paws through the baby burp rags in the top drawer until she finds a small velvet box. I know when she finds it, be-cause her whole body stills for a moment when she does, and then she hiccups as she pulls it out of the drawer. Like it's the most precious thing in the world, she gently pries open the box to see the three rings nestled in the pillows.

"There are three?" she asks.

"The big diamond is the one that I wanted to give you," I tell her. "The little band with the diamonds all around it is for you to wear at work, so the big one doesn't tear your gloves and get in the way. And the solid band, I'm afraid I have to keep for a bit longer. It matches mine, and when I give that one to you, you will be mine forever."

"I'm already yours forever," she breathes. "But I'm happy to let you carry it for a little while."

"Good, baby," I say quietly. "Now come over here so I can put that on your finger, and then kiss me."

"Oh yeah?" she asks playfully.

"Oh yeah," I answer her with all seriousness.

She does not hesitate to move into the room to me, and I love it every time she does it. It will never get old. Tears are still shining in her eyes as she hands me the box, and I slide onto her finger the band with the two-carat emerald-cut diamond that shows the world she's my one and only and I would do anything for her. I lift her hand to my lips and kiss just above the ring.

And then I scoot over, because this chair is huge and awesome, and it's perfect to hold both of my girls while we watch the sun rise on a perfect Saturday morning. Emma scoots in next to me, and I wrap my arm around her.

"I love you, Lee," she says.

"Pleased as punch, honey, because I love you too," I say, making her chuckle a little before I give her the words I have every day since she came back to me, and I hope I always will. "Thank you for giving me everything I ever wanted."

the end

Thank you so much for reading HUSH LITTLE BABY. If you want to know more about the Goodnite and O'Connell family, you can start Claire and Wes's story for FREE with TELL ME A STORY. And if you want to see more of the Lee and Wes bromance, you can find them in The Presidential Affair Series. And grab the conclusion to Emma and Lee's story, DON'T SAY A WORD.

PLAYLIST

Hotel Key—Old Dominion

Rumor—Lee Brice

Whiskey Glasses—Morgan Wallen

Dancing with a Stranger—Normani and Sam Smith

Consequences--Camila Cabello

Every Storm—Gary Allan

Never Really Over—Katy Perry

What If I Never Get Over You—Lady Antebellum

Lonely Eyes—Chris Young

Whatever it Takes—imagine Dragons

To hell and back—Maren Morris

don't say a word

it's all my fault

The smell of sulfur fills my nostrils, and smoke sears my lungs. The heavy weight of the rifle in my hands is like second nature to me. I could carry it in my sleep. During training, I probably did.

But it's the eyes that chill me to the bone in the middle of this hot desert.

I don't know how the intel had gone so bad. I know it happens, but not like this. One minute, the mission was going to plan, and the next, the world exploded. Spurts of gunfire can be heard all around me, but it's the screams that ring in my ears.

"Fuck, fuck, fuck!" I hear Adams scream through the comms in my ear. "They're dead. They're all dead."

And he's right. They're all dead. Every last one of them. I was helpless to prevent this, but still I feel like I should have. It's as bad as if their blood was directly on my hands.

The smoke burns my throat as I turn to the left and see Emma's blonde-and-pink hair, her blue eyes open and watching me, her beautiful body mutilated, because I was in her life.

"No!" I shout.

But the eyes of the dead scream that this is all my fault.

"It's all my fault," I mumble. My throat is raw from the smoke inhalation and the screams echo in my ears, but still I know that that's not right, right?

"That's right," a familiar voice coos. "It's all your fault."

"My fault."

"Yes, Captain Goodnite. It's your fault and now you have to pay."

"It was you," I gasp as I fade in and out of consciousness. "It was all you."

"Yes," they laugh. "It was all me."

"Not my fault."

"Oh no, it's very much your fault and now you're going to die."

My name is Captain Liam Goodnite with the George Washington Township Police Department and it looks like I'm about to die.

Too bad I wasn't ready to go but I guess it's like they say, "Life's a bitch and then you die."

about jennifer rebecca

Jennifer is a thirty something lover of words, all words: the written, the spoken, the sung (even poorly), the sweet, the funny, and even the four letter variety. She is a native of San Diego, California where she grew up reading the Brownings and Rebecca with her mother and Clifford and the Dog who Glowed in the Dark with her dad, much to her mother's dismay.

Jennifer is a graduate of California State University San Marcos where she studied Criminology and Justice Studies. She is also a member of Alpha Xi Delta.

10 years ago, she was swept off her feet by her very own sailor. Today, they are happily married and the parents of a 9 year old and 7 year old twins. She lives in East Texas where she can often be found on the soccer fields, drawing with her children, or reading. Jennifer is convinced that if she puts her fitbit on one of the dogs, she might finally make her step goals. She loves a great romance, an alpha hero, and lots and lots of laughter.

stalk her

Website
JenniferRebeccaAuthor.com

Newsletter
JenniferRebeccaAuthor.com/Newsletter

Facebook
facebook.com/JenniferRebeccaAuthor

Twitter
@JenniRLreads

Instagram
@JenniRLreads

BookBub
bookbub.com/authors/jennifer-rebecca

Book+Main
bookandmainbites.com/users/22594

Dangerous Dames Facebook Group
facebook.com/groups/JRDangerousDames

ALSO BY JENNIFER

The Liam Goodnite Series
Hush Little Baby
Don't Say a Word

The Claire Goodnite Series
Tell Me a Story
Tuck Me in Tight
Say a Sweet Prayer
Kiss Me Goodnight

A Presidential Affair
The Senator's Secret
Caught by the Chief of Staff
The Press Secretary's Passion

The Funerals and Obituaries Series
Dead and Buried
Dead and Gone
Dead and Deceived
Dead and Wed
I Met a Girl, a Funerals Prequel

The Murder on Ice Series
Attack Zone
Layback

The Southern Heartbeats
Stand
Joy
Whiskey Lullaby
Mercy
Just a Dream
Church Bells

Standalones
Trap: A Salvation Society Novel
Dark Horse: A Driven World Novel

ACKNOWLEDGEMENTS

THANK YOU! THANK YOU! THANK YOU!

THANK YOU SO MUCH! For everyone who has patiently (and not so patiently) waited for Lee's book. For everyone who came with me from romcom to suspense, for everyone who loved Claire and Wes so much that you had to know what happened with Lee. I couldn't have done this without you.

THANK YOU ALYSSA! For everything. For the pretty covers, for laughing it off when I send you pretty pictures and ask you to make it creepy, for fielding crazy phone calls where I'm like, I have this idea, for everything. From the first to the last, it's you and me, kid, and I wouldn't want it any other way.

THANK YOU TRICIA! Without you I would be lost. I'm so thankful you walked into my life and sorted me out. You get me, you fix what I break, and you do it with a smile. You're the best!

THANK YOU KAYLA! "Where you goin' lookin' like a slut?" Without you this entire book would probably be illegible. Your sidebar comments keep me laughing. I promise to try and stop rinsing chicken. No guarantees though.

THANK YOU ALYSSA, STACY, EMMA, AND ANDREA! For kicking my ass when I wanted to quit. This was a hard book to write and I struggled. Thank you for keeping me focused and reminding me what's important.

AND ALWAYS LAST BUT NEVER LEAST…

THANK YOU SEAN! We spent a lot of the time I was writing this book apart. Let's not do that again. I missed you a lot. You're my person, my bestie, my baby daddy. You're the one who keeps me ground while helping me fly. Without you I am nothing, with you I am everything. IT WAS ONLY EVER YOU.

www.ingramcontent.com/pod-product-compliance
Lightning Source LLC
Chambersburg PA
CBHW021136110726
47900CB00002B/382